Prais

## PLAIN AIR: SKETCHES FR

T0023318

By the end of this collection, you've been to Winesburg, Indiana. You can recall its businesses and its citizens and whatever it is that is each person's personal business— what makes them tick, individually—what makes them get up in the morning to try, again, to live with themselves and with each other—what makes the many of them so very individual in these vivid and intricate snapshots of their souls.

— **Molly Gaudry**, *We Take Me Apart*

Michael Martone is our curator of community, our impresario of Americana, our chandler of the national flame. *Plain Air* is a wonder. It offers history, wit, and wistfulness all at once—a portrait of a small town made whole by its citizens' laughters and loves.

— **Alyson Hagy**, *Scribe*

*Plain Air* comprises a collage of municipal sadnesses—a poverty of tourists, an amalgam of quiet losses, a blank billboard, an abandoned floss factory, a low-grade apprehension in the face of something already passed, an inventory of forlorn hearts, a docufiction about the exceptional mundane. His Winesburg, Indiana, metaphorizes Flyover as an existential condition with innovative lyricism, meticulous intelligence, and an always-arched eyebrow.

— **Lance Olsen**, *Skin Elegies* and *My Red Heaven*

Michael Martone's *Plain Air* sketches, like prose poems, erupt sharp with insight . . . they're really weird and profound. What more could you want?

— **Terese Svoboda**, *Great American Desert*

*Plain Air* puns and pranks, twists and turns with every new sketch on every page. A play on Sherwood Anderson's classic collection, Martone takes us to Winesburg, Indiana, a post-industrial town with its dying eraser factory, and a cast of characters more alive in their passions, obsessions and idiosyncrasies than any in contemporary fiction. What a great read. I laughed, cried, and was moved by the characters' desire to finally take their place in the intricate web of Winesburg, all the way to their vanishing points in the mural on the post office wall.

— **Mary Swander**, *The Girls on the Roof*

Misfits rejoice! Michael Martone's *Plain Air* gives voice, vision, and velocity to the ordinary and quiet lives of people overlooked, undervalued, and sometimes erased. Each sketch of humanity draws a reader in to the heart of the matter—a curation of basic being. I laughed, I cried, I held my breath, I felt at home. What beautiful little heart bomblettes.

— **Lidia Yuknavitch**, *Thrust*

# PLAIN AIR

# PLAIN AIR

Sketches from Winesburg, Indiana

MICHAEL MARTONE

BAOBAB PRESS

All images sourced from Wikimedia Commons

First Printing

ISBN-13: 978-1-936097-42-5
ISBN-10: 1-936097-42-7
Library of Congress Control Number:
2022933039

Baobab Press
121 California Ave
Reno, Nevada 89509
www.baobabpress.com

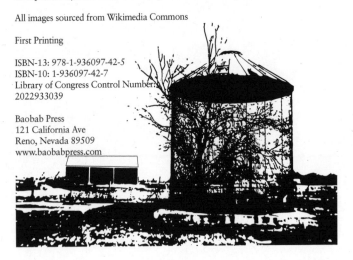

*Note on the Cover:* An antique Hog Oiler from the author's extensive collection. Although the time of pasturing hogs has long passed, Michael Martone recalls fondly the squeals of his (once extensive) herd of swine in harmony with the squeaks of the various therapeutic impliments happily in use. The Hog Oilers were, at one time, brightly painted, but now they have acquired a patina of rusts that, to his aging eyes, still radiate an aesthetic, though hushed, charm.

For Joyelle McSweeney
"It is a sublime site: a site of soaring flights
and subterranean swoons."

# SKETCHES

"I walked in the meadows of green grieving for my life . . ."

— Ivan Turgenev,
*Sketches from a Hunter's Album*

# GREATER WINESBURG, INDIANA

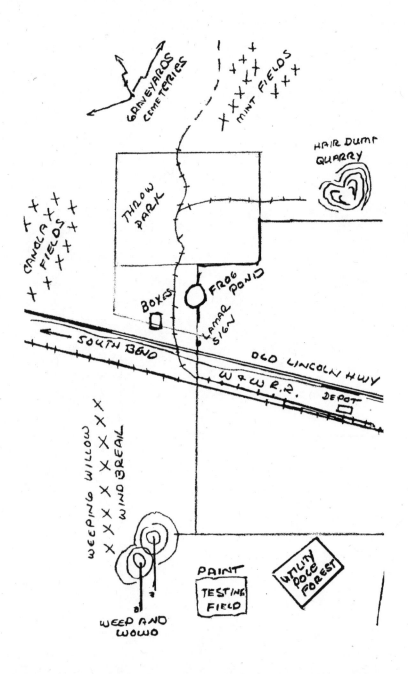

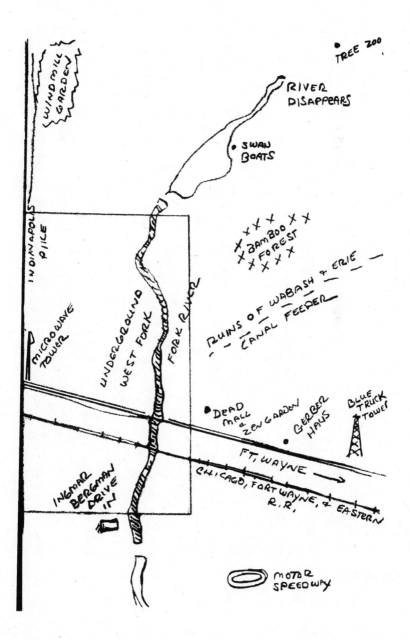

# WINESBURG, INDIANA - CITY LIMITS

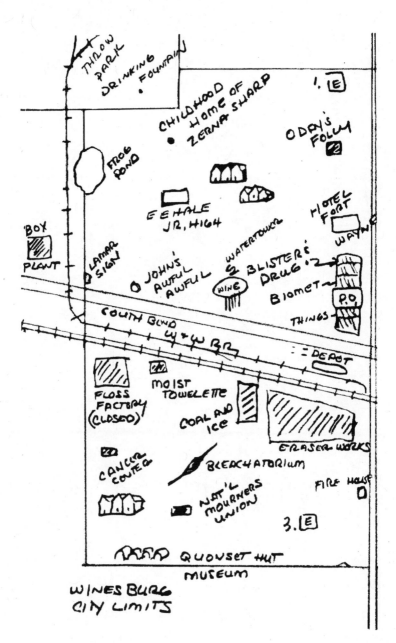

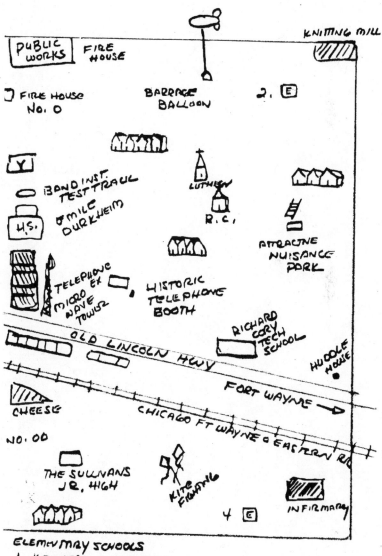

# THE CITY MANAGER: AN INTRODUCTION

The town of Winesburg operates under the weak-mayor system, always has. I am the city manager, a creature of the council charged by the council, five elected members, to keep the trash trucks running on time. There aren't too many other municipal services to attend to. The fire department is volunteer. The county provides the police. There are the sewers of the town, and I maintain them myself. I also conduct the daily public tours. The sewers of Winesburg are vast, channeling one branch of the Fork River through underground chambers and pools roofed with vaulted ceilings tiled with ceramic-faced bricks. The sewers were the last public works project of the Wabash and Erie Canal before the canal bankrupted the state of Indiana. I mentioned tours but there aren't that many tourists. I walk through the tunnels alone, my footsteps on the paving stones echoing. The drip, drip, drip of the seeping water. The rapid splashing over the riprap. There is the landfill as well to manage, the heart-shaped hole where the fossil-rife limestone of the sewers was quarried, punched in the table-flat topography of a field north of Winesburg. We are located on the drained sandy bed of an ancient inland sea. Sea birds from the Great Lakes find their way to the pit, circle and dive down below rim, emerging with beaks stuffed with human hair, for their nests, I guess. Indiana has complicated laws concerning the disposing of cut hair. Much of the state transships its hair here. A thriving cottage industry persists, that of locket making, using the spent anonymous hair to simulate the locks of a departed loved one. The lockets are afterthoughts, fictional keepsakes. The locket makers can be seen rummaging through the rubbish of the dump, collecting bags of damp felt. Winesburg was the first city in the country to install the emergency 911 telephone number. J. Edward Roush, Member of the House of Representatives, was our congressman and was instrumental in establishing the system. What's your emergency? I manage that too, taking a shift, at night usually, in the old switching room, to answer the calls of the citizens of Winesburg who more often than not do have something emerging. But not an acute emergency but more a chronic unrest. An anxiousness. Not a heart attack but a heartache. I listen. The switches, responding to the impulse of someone somewhere dialing, tsk and sigh and click. I manage. I am the city manager.

I am not sure what to do with all the cease-and-desist orders I duly received for the town of Winesburg. I am not sure I understand how to cease and desist the steeping municipal sadness here. It is not as if I or anyone here can help it. Years ago, Fort Wayne, the state's second largest city 40 miles to the east, decided to exhume its dead and to become, like San Francisco, free of cemeteries and graveyards. The consequence of the decision was transporting its remains to multiple planned necropoli on the outskirts of Winesburg. The newly dead arrive daily, carried by a special midnight-blue fleet of North American Van Lines tractor-trailers, escorted up the Lincoln Highway by the Allen County Sheriff's Department. I must admit, it is our biggest industry, bigger than the floss factory, the eraser works, and the cheese plant. We tend. We tend the dead. And the funereal permeates this place in the way Fluoxetine, in all it manifestations, saturates the sewers of Winesburg, the spilled and pissed SSRIs of the citizenry, sluicing into the water table beneath the fossil seabed of an ancient extinct inland sea. Our deathly still suburbs. Our industrious dust. Our subterranean chemistry. Our tenuous analog telephony. Our thin threads of wistful connection. What am I to do? How am I to cease, desist? Manage?

# KEN OF KEN'S CAMERA

Every fall, I visit all the schools in Winesburg to make the pictures. I make the class pictures. I make the individual pictures of each individual student. I make the pictures of the teachers. And even the staff (the janitors, the lunch ladies, the secretaries, the crossing guards, the school nurses), I make their pictures too. I take my camera to The Emile Durkheim High School (the public school), St. Edward the Confessor Roman Catholic School, Martin Luther Lutheran School. Every year, I make all the pictures in all these schools. I make the pictures for the Richard Corey technical school and the Edward Everett Hale, and The Sullivans junior high schools. And I make pictures for the elementary schools (Lincoln, Garfield, McKinley, and Kennedy). Every fall, I make a lot of pictures. And each sitting gets four takes (at least). Everyone gets four tries to make the picture I make come out right.

My wife, Clare, works with me in all the schools on the day we make the pictures. She brings with her the big tackle box of make-up, the jars of hair gel and cans of hair spray, the bobby pins and barrettes, and plenty of mirrors. We don't tell the subjects but the mirrors are trick ones, just a little bit, to flatter their faces, make them thinner, smoother, younger, older. My wife hands out the free hard-rubber pocket combs imprinted with "Ken's Camera Studio" on one side of the handle and "Ace" on the other. She watches the students in the hallway outside the door to the backstage of the cafetoriums where I have set up my temporary studio. All of the children combing and combing their hair, licking their fingers to smooth down cowlick after cowlick. I can hear my wife calm them down. You are lovely, she says. You have a beautiful smile. She says, this is your best side. I believe that school photograph day creates more anxiety than any test. It is after all, a measure of who they have become, all the making-up of the lives they are making-up captured here at this moment. I hear her coax and cajole as I set up the scoop lights and strobes, charge the batteries, adjust the backdrop (it is silver white for all the school pictures though back at the studio I have a variety of backgrounds—the Grand Canyon, the heavy red velvet drapery, the bookshelf filled with books, the end zone of the old RCA Dome), organize the rolls of film (I still use film) with the charts filled with the names of the students waiting outside. Heaven forbid that Ken of Ottumwa would mix up the photographs, caption one picture with the wrong name. No, the kids as they arrange their hair, as they button and unbutton their blouses and shirts, as they remove their glasses, as they smile hard at each other examining each other's teeth—they carry with them a slip of paper with their name and address and a serial number for me to match with the four frames (at least!) that will be allotted to them. The money is in the packages I sell to them—all the different combinations of 8x10s, 5x7s, 3 1/2 x 5s, the wallet sizes, the size for grandparents who will frame the portraits, the postage stamp size for trading with friends. None of the packages make any sense. Everyone always ends up with too many of at least one kind. They get proofs. The four (at least) poses where they try, try, try, try to picture the you that is you (my motto). There is always one half-lidded take or one with the eyes closed altogether, one all a pout when she wanted to smile, one all teeth when he wanted to be tight lipped. Don't get me started on cheese, on the banter I must recite day in and day out, the counting up to the moment I trip the shutter, the stutter as the lights flashing hit the subject. How I must prop him up again as he blinks uncontrollably. How I nicker at her as her irises gyrate and jump. The confusions of my lefts and your rights, the jumbling of movable body parts (the eyes looking up, the chin down, the head turned, the shoulder pulled back). And the smile, smile, smile, smile. The look here, look here, look here, look here. My wife Clare also helps the seniors with the break front formal gowns, the fake strand of pearls, the tuxedo bib, and clip-on bow. The costumes are soaked through by the end of that day's shooting, and we spray it down with the same stuff they use for shoes at the bowling alley. Recently, the anxiety in line has gotten even more compounded and confused as most of the students (even the kindergarteners) carry surreptitious cell phones bundled with their own digital cameras. They are not supposed to have them in school but in the hallway milling, waiting, nervous, bored, their teachers distracted by their own vanities, they turn on their phones, flipping them up like old-fashioned compact mirrors accompanied by little songs twinkling like old music boxes. They make each other's pictures. They make pictures of each other. They make pictures of each other making pictures. They make pictures of each other making pictures of each other. And then (I know it) they begin sending the pictures they have made to each other. I can hear the phones ringing, singing, buzzing, clicking as they receive the pictures. I can feel them, the pictures, being sent in the air around me like the floating after-images of all the real pictures I make of the same children on the spinning piano stool in front of the silver-white background strobing on the excited filmy film of my retina. Back in the dark room I drift around in the dark feeling my way around, around the vats of chemicals, the boxes of paper. I crack open the yellow canisters of spent film like eggs. I spool up rolls and rolls and rolls and rolls of film, bathing them like bars of soap in soapy water. The filmstrips spiral and drip-dry in viney jungle clumps around the room. I spend days enlarging the negatives onto the undeveloped swatches of blank paper. My wife Clare helps me here in the dark in the flashing light of the enlarger enlarging, in the diffuse candling safety light. I make pictures the old way with the sweet smelling chemicals and the balsamic fixing baths, the big stop clocks ticking always ticking, the squeegee squeegeeing. Clare, my wife, and I do some dodging and burning, some over- and underexposing. We crop. We pull focus. I watch her making the pictures, all the techniques of retouching, smoothing the surface of a forehead, plucking an eyebrow, smoothing a cheek, pearling a tooth. She drips a dollop of white paint in an eye recreating the flash of my lights when the picture was made. All of this to give depth to the flat flat flat flatness of the pictures. Shadows and perspective, chiaroscuro with the airbrush's air compressor hissing hissing. We score with the wax pencil. We measure the grainy graininess of the flesh, our eyes pressed into the loops. What will they become? These thems? What will we make of them? Make of themselves? I know one day (if we stay in the business) I will need to switch over to the digital pixels, the alternating codes, the electronic genetics, the ones and o's. But, for now, we watch together (under the safety light) the incubation, the development, the emergence, the revelation of each face, face, face, face, before our eyes, beginning with their eyes opening, opening in the depthless depths of those white white fields.

16

# MARIO TALARICO'S PEONIES

My favorite variety is the Eleanor Roosevelt. I am very conscientious in the spring. I stake and cage the plants. I am careful to deadhead the side branching buds to lessen the weight. I know, you are thinking about the ants, but I don't mind the ants. The ants are as drunk as I am on waiting for those buds to bloom. In the winter I review all the catalogs but I always go back to the Eleanor Roosevelt. Most people think the peonies wilt in the heat, but that is not the case. Peonies are heat tolerant. No, what they need is cold. The crowns need to be frozen, frozen solid. I take no chance. I mulch my peonies through the winter with snow and more snow. All the snow that falls I shovel onto the dormant beds. When it doesn't snow, I'll head down to Ed Harz's Standard Station and retrieve bags of ice to pile on the crowns. It's the tradition in Indiana to plant peonies in rows along the driveway or next to the white siding of the garages and they do look good that way, that peony green of the leaves, that exploding splatter of red. But I have planted my peonies in drifts, the icy pale pink blossoms piling up together, a dream of winter.

# THE PLUMANNS SISTERS' LUSTRON HOUSE

We were both math teachers at the Emilè Durkheim High School. Retired now. Retired into our lovely Lustron bungalow on Languor Lane. Years ago, all the steel pieces arrived by rail on flat cars shipped from the U.S. Steel plant in The Region. We had our classes assemble the components, a geometry lesson we believed, all the prefabricated polygon parts unfolding on the new lawn while the concrete slab was still curing. Now we live inside this complicated equation expressing these extreme tolerances, in the embrace of an engineering that we see every day all around us. This house generates its own magnetic field so that birds on their migrations deflect their vectoring, tangential, radial tuned turnings overhead. Our home is one big attraction, and every inch of wall, ceiling, even the floor is covered by magnets usually reserved for refrigerators. It's another kind of calculus, the big puzzle of fitting together the mosaic of these attractive attracting bits of polarized flare. At night we hear the thousands and thousands of magnets move, jostle a little bit here and there, throb and pulse, attract and repel all around us, foiling us, our arms around each other, some kind of proof at the end of each day, beneath the steel sheets where beneath us, the steel springs of our steel bed are still singing.

# CHARLES AULT, THE LAST LION OF WINESBURG

Once, there was a big chapter of Lions, a pride indeed. We did a lot for the eyes. I still have a garage full of old frames. We managed corneas, arranged trips to New Jersey to pick up a seeing eye dog or two. The Lions dwindled and, as they died, one by one, their eyes were all harvested, our own kind of coin for the ferryman. Lying there in state, decked out in blue and gold, their lids folded over the empty sockets were soldered down with super-glue. I stood at ease in my pleated garrison cap and formal white cotton gloves, overseeing the viewing. I have gotten too old to bare the pall let alone the coffin. I am everyone's honorary now, the Last Lion. We still meet once a month at the Coney Island. I ring the bell, hand out fines. There is only old business. At home, I have all the empty old glass-globed gumball machines. Once, we stationed these machines around the town, everywhere dispensing the gum balls that, now that I think about it, suggested eyes, pickled perhaps, packed in a jar. I look deep into the empty globes now and can see in the glass the reflection of my gaze distorted there and lost in the layers of all that invisibleness caught up inside.

# MARGARET WIGGS'S DUE DATE STAMP

I can't help myself. I've been the librarian at the Little Turtle Branch for next to forever. I was here when we switched to the bar codes, the scanning wands, the stuttering printer spitting out the little chits of paper. I keep the stamp in the drawer, and I do slip my hand inside without thinking and handle the handle, finger the clicking notched wheel that advances the date and days. Needing to knead the mechanism in the dark there beneath the desktop. It is quiet in the library. Patronage has really fallen off as most of Winesburg scrolls on their own through the pages of their handheld devices. I dial through the dates in the dark, travel into the past, the future. After closing, I dim the lights. I focus a task light on an old foxed checkout card and stamp the stamp. There still is a residue of old ink. The numbers, letters are ghosts, and then after another stamp, a ghost of a ghost, overdubbing the overdue.

# THE COUNTY EXTENSION AGENCY'S EXPERIMENTAL BAMBOO PLOT

We knew right away we should not have done it, planted the bamboo. It shoots up. Blame the rhizomes, the threading roots that root and knit together just beneath the skin, underground so that you can't mulch it to mute the growth. It spreads and spreads. Look at it grow, a great green cloud, a graphic depiction of climate change, bamboo absorbing all that excess carbon infused in the air, a great green cough. We thought this grass, the largest grass, could supplant that mutant one we call corn. Bamboo makes a fine pickle. A relish. It can be eaten whole. Flooring. Biomass. But it didn't catch on. The cat was out of the bag and the stuff just spread. We can't stop it though we make gestures to. The burns. The chemicals. The harvests every other day. Secretly we are much amazed by bamboo. Bamboozled by bamboo in fact. How it succeeds as all our agricultural experiments fail, a crop of unintended consequences. The other day I found a sprout of it, a golden spike, slicing through the concrete there. I look out the window and I swear the grove has taken two steps closer to envelope our little station here in this now perennial shade.

# NED SHOOTS THE SUN

I don't really "shoot" the sun. "Shoot" is another way
of saying I am taking a sighting. My sextant, you might
gather, is homemade. You will find me each day at noon
making noon on my backdoor deck. I have charts that
Doris down at the AAA special ordered for me from a
ship chandler in Baltimore. I make my calculations, and
I make my position as my backdoor deck, docked in the
port city of Winesburg, Indiana. Over all these years,
I've barely budged. I've barely budged though the earth
has moved. Or is it the sun moving. Most of my life Indiana did not participate in Daylight Saving but now it
does. Making daylight, saving hay. I need to recalibrate
my chronometers, the compass spinning in the binnacle.
Doris adores me because I refuse to use the Global Posi-
tioning Satellites that circle overhead. She provides me
new old maps that come in cardboard tubes that I will
incorporate into my more and more complex instruments
for my "shootings". I am adrift in the wreck of my backyard, waiting to shoot today's sun, navigating by this do-
it-yourself dead reckoning.

# MY GRANDFATHER'S RIDDLE

My grandfather's riddle appeared again out in the garden once the snow melted. There it was—a lozenge of a warped wooden moon mired in the mud. I had forgotten it was there, that it has always been there. I bet its screen is all rusted out. Sifting, he spent hours back there sifting that rough dirt fill. Winesburg is smack dab in the middle of a glacial plain, and the dirt that granddad riddled was dirt that had been snowplowed to Indiana from regions half a world away. The glaciers themselves are a kind of sieve, sorting boulders from rocks, sanding them all into pea pebbles that remain in the creases of the rusted old riddle, a kind of fruit or fruit's stone. My grandfather would serve up the leavings to me in the riddle, telling me where they came from, that world away, how the grit wound up at our feet. After all the sifting, they would wind up, a random wreck, sprayed on my dresser top, a dresser I need to re-stain, that was my grandfather's and that has come down to me here on this fine fine earth.

# MY FLAT TOP

Don Cofelt, my barber, has a level he keeps under the ultraviolet light back there, a level with little bubbles inside clear tubes that bounce back and forth between scored marks. I watch them in the mirror as they percolated back and forth and find, well, their level. "That's got it," Don says when we've got it—my hair clipped in a smiling chevron that scallops into the dome of noggin—horizontal. I like to say to anyone who'll listen that I've had my ears lowered. Don has a sign taped to the mirror that says, "Many men think they are being cultivated when they are only being trimmed." It is cold in winter. I travel, hatless with my new hair, through the streets of Winesburg. The wind skids over my scalp as if it is steel wool finishing my shiny pate. Burnished. "Flat Top" is also something they call an aircraft carrier, and as I navigate my way home I imagine launching and recovering my thoughts. Whole wings of thinking circling, flying in formation on patrol around my head, alert, dauntless, searching for what is out there just beyond that endless horizon up ahead.

# TAB GALLENBECK, PUBLIC WORKS

I wish that I could know how much salt to order each season. I know that some folks have a joint that twitches or head that aches when a storm's brewing, the pressure dropping, the wind coming about. I'm going to need 250 cubic yards of rock salt, 575 cubic yards of sand. It is better to have too much than too little I always say. Don't you think the drifts of salt look like (could be) drifts of snow? In the year of little snow, of no snow, these salt mounds will have to stand in for snow. As the storm approaches, the temperature falls, I load up the pick-up, shovel in the salt on the rusting bed in back. Daughter Wendy drives. I get into a rhythm in the back, scooping up a heap of salt, fanning it out on the road, rolling aft of the tailgate. I like the way the crystals bounce and scrabble, how they sow themselves into windrows, waiting for the snow to come. The streets of Winesburg are silent. Folks burrowing in. I feel the ache in my arms, my back. The pressure falling. We weave through the stains of light and shadow that the streetlights cast. It smells like snow. It smells like snow and salt.

# THE SNOW FENCES OF WINESBURG

I miss the wooden snow fences, red cedar slats. They have disappeared, replaced by these orange plastic nets. I don't know who does this, puts up the snow fences here and there all over Winesburg every fall. They work, knocking the snow out of the gale, the gale itself generated, I guess, by a kind of fence, the barrier between the great lake and land that dumps the snow out of the rolling clouds of the deep gray sky. I joke with my wife that if they just don't put up the snow fences it won't snow as if the fences tempt the snow. It's a joke, you see. I am mixing up the effect and cause. But still after the long winter and all that howling snow-choked wind, I keep saying to myself, "Take them down. Take them down. Take them down." That will stop the snow. The snow fences are the trigger. The lure. It makes me think of those South Sea Islands where the cults built decoys of airplanes to attract the cargo. The fences bring on the snow, and it snows. And what little sun is left throws that corrugated shadow on the bleached drifted ground—nets of nets the new fences cast. Better than the prison bars of the old fences, I guess.

# BUD'S KOMET'S PUCK

I grew up in Fort Wayne on Wells Street at St. Vincent Villa, a Catholic orphanage in those old days. Out back there was a three-story cement statue of the Blessed Mother us kids would climb. I have no idea if it is still there. The place has been turned into a Y, I think. I don't know what it is now. I don't get back there much at all. This puck's all that's left of my adventures back then. Back then, high school kids in do-gooder clubs would troop a whole bunch of us out to events, score points, I guess, with who-ever keeps track of such things. Basketball, lots of basket-ball games. Legion baseball. And Komet hockey at the Memorial Coliseum. It was okay to get out from time to time, blow the stink off of us, but we never stopped being orphans. And those high school kids just when they were starting to feel good about the good deeds they were doing finally couldn't make out hides nor tails of us urchins. "Get me a puck," I'd say to one of them, his eyebrows all arched up. "Tell 'em we're orphans. They'll give you a puck if they know we're orphans." And they would. Everybody feeling bad all around wanted to feel good. That was the situation back then. Now, here I sit in Winesburg, deep in hockey season. That's the Komets playing, broadcast on WOWO. Icing, I never understood icing. I bet there is snow all caught up in the cement folds of Mother Mary's veil. This puck, I pretended, was some perverse communion wafer I lodged in her icy mouth. It never melted, of course, like the real thing did, but glowed there like the lost frozen hunk of dust it was.

# BOBBI BODINKA'S RUBBINGS

My mother used to take in ironing, and I grew up watching her iron in the living room so she could watch the soaps on the TV while she did it. She let me sprinkle the wrinkled shirts, the crumpled slacks. We used an old empty 7-UP bottle stoppled with a holey nozzle I'd shake the water out through. I liked to watch the way the wrinkles and creases disappeared as Mother bore down on the iron and turned the water into steam, a steam that sizzled and sang. Outside, through the window over the television, the world in winter Winesburg had been ironed flat. White snowy fields folded into snowy field after snowy field. There were times as she fluffed and arranged the shirts on the board she would forget to set the iron on its edge and the hot plate would singe and stain the pad, the shadow adding a kind of depth to all that flatness. I think of that now years later when I take the patterns off the manhole covers with my artistic rubbings. I sell the results at the farmers markets in Fort Wayne. The first impression I took was off my mother's gravestone, a slab, flat against the grass. As I pressed and scrubbed, scrubbed and pressed the white paper, the words and picture—the anvil shape of hands folded in prayer—emerging, I found I remembered more and more of those afternoons with my mother, the snow outside sifting over the sheets of snow, the sighs of steam, the smoldering smell of the stalled iron on the singeing top of the ironing board on top of those tottering, scissored legs.

# THURSDAY

I am pretty sure that it is Thursday out there. That looks like a Thursday sky doesn't it? It does doesn't it? They call this window a picture window and the picture it is picturing is "Thursday". I am pretty sure that it is Thursday. I have trained myself to notice the way Thursday looks in Winesburg. I don't look at the calendars or the clocks. I've trained myself to pay attention to the Thursday-ness of the day. The sky especially, the way the clouds maneuver in the latter half of the week, the way the blue is steeped. It's tricky, Thursdays. Thursdays, I have found, can last a long time out there. Days can go by. But all those days are Thursdays too, Thursdays auditioning for Friday, trying Friday on for size.

# THE LAMAR SIGN ON THE OLD LINCOLN HIGHWAY

We can't remember the last time the sign on the outskirts of Winesburg last advertised anything. We don't really understand why the sign company itself doesn't use the sign to advertise there is this sign to use to advertise. The emptiness is mesmerizing. There are times that the whiteness of the billboard seems luminous. Some nights it gives off a light, we swear, more than reflection, a kind of glow that appears to emanate from deep within, a chemical reaction perhaps, a glaze of phosphorescent moss perhaps, symbiotic with the lime in the whitewash maybe. Maybe. It is a kind of camouflage, mimicking the exact shade of atmospheric exhaustion that envelopes us, evaporating everywhere hereabouts, where the blue has been leeched out of the sky, a perpetual not sky sky, that the sign is a sign of and for. We all go by it daily, going and coming, and we have all glossed it, think we know each etched wrinkle of the crazed bleached surface floating there as if it mirrors the crimped creases ironed into our own cortexes, a no-brainer. One day, we may gather there, promote the structure, a festival maybe, celebrating the sign as our sign, the sign that has come to represent that something something about us all.

# SANDOR REEVES'S EXTENSION CORD

There must be a way, mathematically, to describe the coiling of these cords and the algebra of the knots and kinks that spring up in the endless looping I go through storing them, but I was (am) bad at math, especially the finite kind that is all about permutations and probabilities and odds and ends, odds and ends, yes, I socket together in the Butler Building out back through the long winter where I braid and loop and lasso these extending extensions, all insulated in shades of orange, yellow, neon greens, while it snows and snows outside, coating the general vicinity of Winesburg, Indiana, a skin of snow that extends in lake effected bands all the way to Fort Wayne, there, off in the arching distance where I see its lights electroplating the lowering clouds, creating this other effect that warps the distance into arches, dull glowing domes as I wrap another length of wire round my elbow and into the crook my palm creates and back to the bend of the elbow; miles, I have miles and miles now of these candy-colored tangles that, one day, I will fit together, length by length, letting it find its way east, to the source, to some solution, to the light at the end of the light.

# DEB SANDERS'S ETCH-A-SKETCHES

It was *THE* Christmas present to have in 1960. I was five, and the next Christmas I used it to write Santa a note and left it there next to the plate of cookies and the carrots for the reindeer. That was the last year I believed. The cookies were gone and carrots half-eaten and my message all erased and Santa, or someone I was supposed to believe was Santa, made an attempt to write something back, the lines like cracks in the glass. Years have gone by. I stopped writing notes. I stopped drawing the pictures, all scratchy and nervous lines slipping off at odd angles when my fingers slipped on the dials. I've spent years, finally, going back and forth, back and forth, up and down, rubbing away the silver coating line by line, revealing, as the dust sifted away, the elegant mechanism beneath the metallic film, the stylus and the articulated beams, cables, and springs. Every time the apparatus appeared (and there were many times, I bought new ones after I erased the old ones) I was always surprised that the magic that seemed so evident before us could be so patently peeled away. I've hung the transparent shells now on the walls around my windows, windows framed by windows. In the winter the glass frosts over, and I find I take my finger and touch the cold cold, a kind of curser, and melting away the cataract of ice, a little peephole there and then another, that then expands as my finger etches out a horizontal streak across a pane, exposing the predictable geometry of wintery Winesburg beyond. It passes the time.

# RON'S LAWN ROLLER

He wants us to borrow it. It is an ungainly thing, the lawn roller, but Ron insists. He rolls his roller over to our lawn to demonstrate the proper technique of how to roll a lawn. "It is as easy as that," he says after he has gone over and back over the lawn. The lawn, after he is done, looks like it has been painted two shades of green—green and greener. It doesn't look all that easy—the roller is concrete, for goodness sake—and old Ron, he's huffing and puffing after pushing that stone this way and that. We know Ron's heart is in the right place. He just wants the lawns of greater Winesburg to look nice. Who doesn't? Ron sits on our front stoop, recovering from his recent exertion, intent on us rolling our lawn with his lawn roller. We know what you are thinking. How hard can it be with the whole landscape from here to the horizon that seems leveled to within an inch of its life, flat as flat can be? But when we are wrangling the roller across our lawn, believe us, where slight declivities, slopes, and inclines are transmitted through the wooden handles. Here, it inches upward. There on the edge of running away down hill. We admit it takes our breath away, our sense of things all flattened, to map the subtle seeming but really gigantic disruptions of degree, the thickness of a blade of grass, differences in altitude between here and here.

# JIM O'DAY'S FOLLY

If anyone ever wants to build anything again here in Winesburg, I'm ready. But no one has wanted to build anything in a long time, so I wait. I wait, tools at the ready. I have all the materials I need to build the building's building structures—the scaffolding and the forms, the struts and braces. They fit together neatly to build towers and the skeletons of walls, and they come apart just as neatly, back into their piles of tubes and joints and platforms and turnbuckles. I wait for the phone to ring. It never rings. I spend my time constructing and tearing down my elaborate skeletons of scaffold. Architects would call these follies—buildings that are built for no other reason than to build them. They are brand new fake ruins, fun to look at but in no way habitable. Though you will see me living up there, I guess, bolting over the monkey bars, this jungle gym. Everyday, I rig a more and more elaborate maze of beams and pipes, cross-braced and buttressed—a building made out of the methods of building buildings. And each night, I take it apart, revealing, once this facade of a facade is torn down, the nothing I was constructing out of the nothing all around me.

# BOB IN THE AIR, SCALING THE OLD MICROWAVE TOWER IN WINESBURG, DISMANTLING THE OBSOLETE DRUMS

I remember hauling these drums up this tower when we were bouncing the antique microwaves around the country. AT&T's long lines came through Winesburg—the shortest route between points A and B, important nodes, junctions. There is a lot of talk about this being the epicenter of the flyover country but back then invisibility itself, this electromagnetic tide, swept right through us, transmitting the ordinary hubbub on its back, radiating. After I unhinge the device, and it lurches down, stalled from falling by Bob on the ground, I have a moment to look out over the unfolding surroundings. Off in all directions I can see the other towers similarly undergoing their own renovations. I wave as if the guy on the tower there intersecting the horizon can see me, the light from the sun bouncing off my palm and undulating its way, carrying the image of the blur of my hand waving, to the receptive lozenges of his own eyes, there to be decoded into a friendly gesture, a warning. A hello, perhaps, but more likely a goodbye.

# JIMMIE D'ANGELO'S OBSERVATORY

I built it myself. It's in my backyard. It is the size of a big doghouse. It is difficult to view the stars in this part of Indiana. The lake generates layers of clouds. I thought the solar collector would be a good idea but. The clouds again. I have a redundancy built in. I've rigged up some old bicycle sprockets, chains and I can crank open the dome on my own. Open up into the occluded night sky of Indiana where even the moon at its fullest, even at perigee, presents only as a dull flashlight cast on the back of a moldy piece of bread. I've forgotten what the stars look like when they are wheeling overhead. What they look like when they are falling. I have gotten good delaminating the overcast, stripping the layers in the cloud cover. Or so I imagine. The clouds, they roil as I light upon them, rearrange the various components of their slack lumpiness. The truth is it gets old looking at the stars and only seeing clouds. I can stand up in my little observatory, my oracular noggin emerging through the slot in the dome. I turn my gaze toward the house, lit from within, search for a glimpse of my wife in a window. The longer I stay out, the more the lights in the house go out as she gets ready for bed. Soon the whole house is in the dark, a shadow of itself. Now that the lights are out, I know she is in some darkened window looking out at me in the dark, my silhouette back lit by the street light behind me, the one I have been trying to get the city manager to extinguish, light pollution, but that now is way beside the point.

# THE WINESBURG CANCER CENTER

We don't get much call here for chemo what with the big
Lutheran Hospital right down the road in Fort Wayne.
After the infusions, folks like to take in the sights of the
big city, maybe stop at Glenbrook before heading back
up 30 to home. We got a deal on the lounge chairs at Kit-
tles near the mall. They are quite comfortable. We often
use them, between the patients, to knit the caps, we have
a closet full, for once the hair sloughs off. We also knit
other things to pass the time, bombing the neighborhood
with our creations. Sweaters for the tulip trees. Cozies for
the fire hydrants. Blankets for the box hedge out front.
The chemicals work, you know, but they are just not very
smart. They drip and steep. Injected, they search through
the body, a circulatory system like yarn, a tangled skein,
looking for the fast-growing cells. That would be the cancer. But hair is fast growing cells. Fingernails. It is nice
here. We try to make it nice. The treatment takes hours.
There are television monitors, movies. Bowls of candy,
squares of chocolate. There is a big picture window that
looks out over the grove of tulip poplars, the state tree of
Indiana, wearing their brightly colored sweaters we have
knit for them. Cardinals like to pull at the sleeves, unrav-
eling the weave. Feathering a nest, I bet. The cardinal is
the state bird of Indiana. Look, the pill caught up in the
reddish bill. Each chemical, in its mushy plastic pillow,
has its own color-coding. That red is that red, threading
through the air, not a blood red but hard candy, finding
its silent red way home.

39

# AMANDA PATCH

It all started innocently enough when I petitioned the Most Reverend Leo, Bishop of the Diocese of Fort Wayne-South Bend to initiate the beatification of Father Herman Heilmann founder of the monastery, Our Lady of the Circumcision, here in Winesburg. Father Herman made a home for his brother fathers, who come from all over the country to this quiet cloistered retreat—a collection of cabins initially converted from the rundown Rail Splitter Motor Court off the old Lincoln Highway—there to study and pray and meditate on that old Old Testament story of Abraham having to sacrifice his son Jacob to establish the covenant with the Lord. I just thought the Father's work needed to be recognized, so in addition to my letter-writing campaign, I convinced my reading group to concentrate on one book, for a year, deeply meditating on the martyrs, spending each meeting discussing a life of a saint we read in Butler's *Lives of the Saints*. It was difficult, to say the least. The litanies of the deaths and the dying, the various methods of torture and the infliction of pain seemed organized in such a way as to demonstrate the excruciating genius of Satan, working through his minions on earth, to exact utter and endless agony. My reading group, made up of several of the neighborhood's ladies and ladies from the church, also met on Wednesdays each spring to follow the March Madness of the basketball tournament, suspending our usual stock club meetings to substitute the brackets for the fine print of the big board. We were, perhaps, predisposed to such communal excitement, some might even say hysteria. As we read and reported on the lives of the saints, our presentations became more elaborate, the distinction between the mere abstract recounting of the material and actually living the lives of the lives of the saints became confused for us, and very soon we became enamored by the very particular narratives of the sainted virgins. We were impressed with the passion of their passion to remain un-deflowered, intact, innocent, and dedicated to Jesus to the point of taking Our Savior as a wedded yet chaste husband. There were (I remember, how could I forget) multiple incinerations at the stake, crucifixions, beheadings, stonings, rapes and sodomies with a variety of implements and animals in an effort to pry from these devoted young women the most special jewel in their possession. It was all quite thrilling. We were moved. The antique prose of the text added a musty patina of gothic authenticity to the recitations of anguish, courage, and ecstatic exultation. All of us, by this time, were far from our own corporeal purity, having given birth to nearly four-dozen children among us. Many of us now were grandmothers as well. We had long suffered both the pangs of birthing and the fandangos of sexual intercourse, procreative and not, at the hands of our husbands and, dare I say, lovers. I am not sure whose idea it was initially, as many of us have used the skilled services of Dr. Minnick for other plastic operative rearrangements, but we somehow reached a consensus that all of us would participate in a kind of tauntine in reverse. We would not so much wait to unstop the cork of a pilfered "liberated" brandy but to stop it all back up again in the first place. You have heard of women's clubs, such as ours, creating calendars of their members photographed tastefully nude, a fundraiser for charity. Our idea was only, we thought, a slight variation on such projects. Perhaps it was Dr. Minnick himself who suggested it, inviting us to consider reconstructive surgeries "down there" commenting that labia reduction is now his most performed and profitable operation, the norming and neatening up, if you will, of the pudenda to the standard folds and tuffs, bolsters and grooves of the ideal cosmetic model. Again, we were thrilled, that such miracles can be performed relatively painlessly in an outpatient setting. But, I do know for a fact, that this would not suit us. We proposed to Dr. Minnick that he attempt to go beyond the mere landscaping of what can be seen but also seek the unseen, to take us back in time. To state it simply—to reattach our long-gone maidenhoods, cinching closed once more the orifice of our experience, virginal once more. And this he did, was anxious to do. Inventing a kind of embroidered helmet for the task, he wove the cap together from multicolored and multi-gauged sutures, a kind of monofilament cartilage tissue. The truth is when we are together now, reading further into the lives of the saints and the endless mortifications of the flesh, we continue to admire, in great detail, during our break for cookies and tea, his handiwork performed on each and every one of us, and how such emendations have delivered us all, strangely beautiful and pristine, one step closer to God.

# A DEEP FAT FRIED BREADED PORK TENDERLOIN FROM JOHN'S AWFUL AWFUL (AWFUL GOOD, AWFUL BIG)

It takes awhile to tenderize the meat. We use the peen end of a ball peen hammer, a hammer I inherited from my grandfather who was a coppersmith, to tenderize the meat in a manner not unlike the forging of the famous samurai swords of Japan, or so I am told, hammering the cut of meat and then folding it back on itself and hammering it flat again and again before it is inserted in the sleeve of the breading, the flour of which I grind myself with a marble mortar and pestle I inherited from my other grandfather, a pharmacist at Blister's Drug in downtown Winesburg, and then the whole concoction is lowered into the deep fat fryer, the basket of which was constructed from a salvaged shopping cart from the abandoned Roger's Market, but most importantly you need to know about the hog itself that, in its demise, gives up its chop, its shoulder, and butt for all the manipulation I have already described, and I do spend weeks wandering the flat Indiana landscape, as flat as a map as big as the thing it represents, as flat as the sandwich that itself, a product of a world of two dimensions, lacking depth, no height, no thickness as it spreads, a sheet of meat that expands to fill this vacuum, this slice so thin it is on the edge of pure nothing, searching for the wild boars of Northern Indiana as they flatten, an optical illusion generated by their camouflage that confuses the foreground from the background, making it difficult, if not impossible, to predate the wily but delicious prey.

# AMY MARGOLIS'S PILE OF LIGHTS

I don't understand the lead. This little tag here saying that I should, after the hours of unknotting the strand from itself, wash my hands. Lead. It seems these lights have been steeped in lead. After hours of threading backwards through all the old coiling of time it took to get here, a kind of rosary in reverse, back through the year it took to create all this confusion, I do unhitch this from that and that this from this there and this that there to there. The strand stretches across the living room, trails behind like a long detachable lizard tail—painted with lead. Perhaps that is it. The color, the green garland green, can—maybe—only be attained by an application of lead. I don't know. The night is a dark cold stone over the dull anvil of Winesburg. I fit the lights into the hedge, adorning the dew, all the time the leaded cord, I can feel it, wants to resume its balled up primitive primeval state. I feel the stars overhead unhinge, ancient catastrophic moments just now sorting themselves out into plumb lines of dirty light.

# ARCHEOLOGY IS A KIND OF DESTRUCTION

Walking home from work, I walk along the west bank of the west fork of the Fork River that flows through Winesburg, Indiana, kicking at this or that shiny object poking up through the mud. The objects thus kicked up? Bottles mostly. "Pop" bottles as we say in the Midwest, oozing the mud, an effervescent stew. I like the old script lettering and the etched groove and rims of the proprietary glass. All these bottles were deposit bottles. You could take them back for the nickel deposit at Rupp and Ottings Market. Who knows where the bottles went from there. Once, I remember, they found one of the retired men who worked as bag boys at the market expired half in half out of the deposit bottle bin. No one had noticed. Everyone thought he was bent over there, rearranging the cases and grates of sticky bottles at the bottom. I take the new find home with me and work to turn the silt inside out, the mud frothing out its mouth in gasping pulsing bleats. Welling, the brew is welling. There is nothing to do with the artifacts now. No taking them back. All the nickels on deposit somewhere, never to be redeemed.

# SEAN (OD) FOR THE EYES

The thing that keeps me up nights is not the cataracts or the glaucoma but the Fuchs's corneal dystrophy. The cells of the endothelium are like little pumps pumping out the excess fluid, and I can see them, one by one, breaking down, the bilge building up in there. In Winesburg we are in the lee of the lake, in the shadow of that eponymous effect, the clogged occluded atmosphere of here. That is to say that after I spend my days orbiting the inner eyes of the citizenry, I walk home through the persistent planet of fog, generated by the flukes of the local obscure geography. To top it off, you can hear the pumps of the Waterworks's substations lifting water seeping out of the various sumps. The streets look treated, wet down to make them look like it's just rained. I flip up the collars of my drenched trench coat, look out of the corner of my eyes, catch a glimpse of myself looking like I am looking in the blinded plate glass, the credits of the movie drizzling down my back.

# THE ALBINO WOODCHUCKS OF WINESBURG

Every morning during the Little Red Barn Show on WOWO, Bob Sievers, the show's personality, calls the dozen troop barracks of the State Police distributed around Indiana. I remember waking up in the dark and listening to the scratchy radio transmission of the sketchy telephone connections while outside it was always snowing, a dust like static of snow. "Any fatalities overnight in The Region, Captain?" Bob would whisper. "No, Bob, no. Quiet night," would come the answer. And then the echoing hang-up and the quick dialing of the next number. And after all the calls to all the corners of the state, Bob turned his attention outside his own window, looking down from the world famous fire escape of WOWO radio and with night vision goggles looked for the herding albino woodchucks of Winesburg as they infiltrated the marshes down by the West Fork of the Fork River, the ghostly animals like ice floes slid over the frosted grass, sifting toward the slushy stream. No one sleeps in Winesburg, it seems. Not me. Not the groundhogs, negative shadows, who seemed to hibernate only in the summer. During the long nights, on this long flat glacial plain, where nothing happens, this happens. This skittish swish and stroll of white fur through the empty streets, a roiling roll of drifts, a scuttle, scraps of paper in the gutters. "You should see this," Bob reports. He thinks he sees them in the shadows, is amazed by their everyday abnormality. The only thing in the whole state worth noting, this solid species of absence.

47

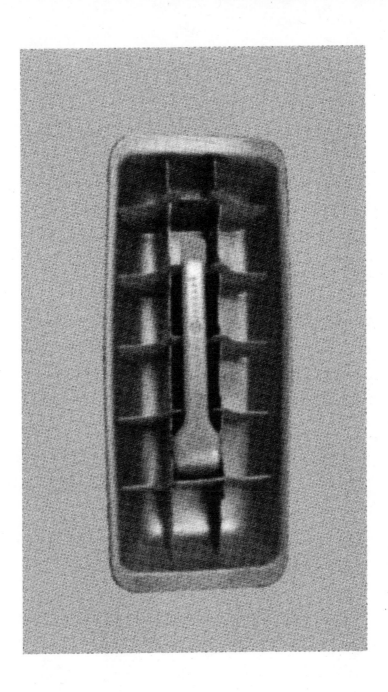

# BLANCHE'S ALUMINUM ICE CUBE TRAY

I have wondered for a long time how to get the air out of ice. I see it in there like a captured cloud under glass, a blown dandelion frozen right before it explodes. I've tried to fill up each section slowly, no splashing to swallow up an emptiness. I let it set, all the bubbles trapped inside working their way through the layers of liquid. But how long to wait? How long does it take to have them percolate to the surface, sift into the surrounding space? Pristine. The solid geometry of transparency. But in each fractured cube I manufacture (I can't help it) another explosion, the air stalled, a smear of a sigh enveloped. The aluminum handle is always encrusted with a new coat of hoary frost that scalds my skin when I crack the botched batch from the tray. I hold them up to the light. One by one, already melting but not disappearing, another mussed mess, fused, fudged, foiled.

# MY FAMILY'S VELVET ROPES

I remember being wakened up early by my mom and dad and tucked into the way back of the station wagon as they drove all over northeastern Indiana salvaging old closed falling down smalltown movie theaters. I think it was their dream, my folks, to open up the long shuttered Damm Theatre in downtown Winesburg. The dawn broke over Indiana like tubes of cursive neon, the burned-out star marquee blinking out, or so I remember it. The theater never opened, and now, mom and dad are long gone. I still make sorties out into the wider world looking for stuff, for the one something that might tie the whole mess of stuff together. I have a lot of red velvet rope and beat up brass stanchions. The ropes breathe out an exhaust of dust, have that old velvet rope smell, the brass brassy. My mom and dad always said that Disney's greatest contribution to entertainment was not the animated movie or the theme park but the line we stood in to get in. It was the way he used these soft saggy ropes to round up his rubes. He invented waiting. We waited, led and leading, forward and reverse through time, passing by, over and over, the strangers who, like us, find themselves lost in this distracting delta of anemic tributaries, thinking we are going, going somewhere soon, there, around that next corner only to find faces again you think you recognize.

# MY HUSBAND'S, CLAUDE BAMBARGER'S, WRECKED WRECKER

While he lived, he ran a wrecker service out on the old Lincoln Highway in Winesburg. The phone rang at all hours. The triple A was our bane. This part of Indiana seems to be a confluence of accidents and unexplained breakdowns. US 30 is a carpet of carpet tacks. Off into the night he would go with his wrecker to winch some-one out of a ditch, fix a flat, jumping to jump the stalled, broke down, lost only to find an airbag exploded, a driver or passenger ejected, the vehicle succumbed to its too high center of gravity. I'd wait up. Smoke on the porch. Watch the stars crash and careen. In the morning, I would take the second wrecker out, looking for him on the county's waste oiled section roads, find him asleep in the cab, the truck picketed with spent, burned-out flares. There was always something broken, something to be fixed. When he died, the other wreckers from all around northeastern Indiana drove over for the funeral. The cops were there too, all the lights blinking. I should get one of them to come and haul that excuse-for-a-truck away. I sit on the porch and smoke, watching it rust, watching the vegeta-tion overtake it. It is an eyesore. There isn't much left to salvage. At this late date, I hate to bother anyone about that old wreck.

# DETECTIVE SGT. GABBIE CLINE, INDIANA STATE POLICE

They look really authentic, the body outlines (there have been a dozen of them now) that have been appearing on the streets, parking lots, and sidewalks of Winesburg. A serial silhouetter, I guess. I should know. I am a profiler for the State Police. I spend my time imaging, trying to get in under the skin, the intention of the malcontent, putting together a narrative of immediate horror. I map the internal dynamics of trauma that bring this particular murderer to this or that crossroad of mayhem. I am pretty good myself outlining the evidence of the body I am investigating in all its awkward stillness. But this, this is something altogether different. There is, at the heart of each drawing, an absence so singular that the gravity of the sketched-out act of violence can't crawl out of that negative space of my contemplation. Maybe it's art. I am afraid it is art, and the perpetrator of these creations will strike again, the residue of loss a sketch, a gesture of ruin always just out of reach.

# THE WINESBURG MOTOR SPEEDWAY

I remember a time when the speedway roared. Dad would take all the neighborhood kids out there, the track lit up, on hot summer nights to see the Sprint Cars and the Midgets zoom in the banks, their shadows spinning around as the cars rounded the curve, whipped through the turns. We knew a kid whose father owned the body shop and drove his own late model stock car, Number 4, permanently dented, it seemed, even though he let us hammer out the dents in his garage the next day. The car, a Dodge, was painted an organ pink and the sheet metal sparked as we pounded it. The oval track turned into a Figure 8 each week for the demolition derbies, the cars driving backward, protecting their engines, crashing into each other's trucks, shedding panels and fenders, the drivers breaking off the broom handles indicating demise, the engines seized, an axle smashed, stalled, and stopped. Action. Everything confused. Who's chasing who backwards and forwards through the infield intersection. T-boned. Tipped over. Drifting. Skidding. Tires smoking. The next day, on our bikes, we would race up and down Runion Street, using the manhole covers at each end of the block, as our pylons to pivot about. We started thinking it was a race but sooner or later lost track of that and then just took aim at each other, thinking no one ever wins but maybe you could avoid losing. The track is a ruin now. And I am the only one left around here of the old gang. Dad's dead. And that other Dad is dead. I like to walk the fraction of the mile left for exercise, that's for sure, but I don't push it. What's the hurry?

# CAPTAIN STEVE "EVEN" STEVEN, 122ND WING INDIANA AIR NATIONAL GUARD

That's me in the A-10. The airplane is a tank killer. Built to hover like a kite over a battlefield, strike like some raptor. I am strapped into a bathtub of titanium, the platform designed to take a beating. That's me accumulating hours, circling over the flat flatness of northeastern Indiana, me and my wingman, scissoring and spiraling over the environs of Winesburg. We target a grazing tractor, imagine that Case is wounded T-72 to be mopped up. That's me on the deck, simulating a gun run. That's me peeling off, the stubby wing control surfaces flexing and flapping. Here I am floating over this blasted landscape, a desert of corn and burned-out barns and toppled silos. If you ask me I will tell you that this is what we are fighting for, always fighting for. That's me snug in the cockpit, on the edge of a stall, tipping the nose over into a spinning dive, imagining, as I fall, in exquisite detail and with telling precision, the havoc I have in my hands.

# BRANDON ZWEIG'S LIFE PRESERVER

You never know. You just never know. I like to be prepared for all eventualities. It's ready to go. I test it monthly to see, in all the humidity of Winesburg, that it retains its buoyancy. And it does. I like to see it floating there in the stagnant ditch all orange and slowly rotating in time, it seems, with the rotation of the earth underneath it. I am attracted to that color. It says "SAFE" to me. It means, "PRESERVED." I heard someplace about the silk of a sari, how it is tested by being able to pull all that yardage through the gauge of a finger ring. I think about that sometimes as I am sitting there in the den watching TV with the lifesaver throbbing in the corner, the stormy light bouncing around the room. I have to keep myself from going over and fitting myself inside that ring, taking it for a spin, trying it on for size.

# DRAKE CAST, GROUND CREW

They let me take the field marker home even though it isn't mine like they let a policeman take home the cruiser after work. It's a perk. You probably would call it lime, the white chalk that the field marker dispenses. But real lime would burn the grass, scorch the ground. It's ground marble dust for real. Marble. Think of that. The stuff of statues. Baseball is the worst. I use an elaborate stencil to sketch out the batter's box and then the first batter up spends all his time rubbing out the lines. The lime goes all over. I don't know why I bother. Football, on the other hand, treats the hash marks and yard lines and out-of-bounds boundaries as if they are some sacred tattoo. I do practice in my backyard after all the games are over. Making a straight line isn't all that hard. Here is the secret—you stretch out a snap line and snap it. You just follow it right along. No, what I practice in my backyard is writing script, my name mostly. I do it with my eyes closed, imagining I am floating overhead like a blimp over a big stadium, looking down on all the cursive application stirring up the dust in my backyard. When I finish, I really can't judge how well I've done. I do need some elevation, a bit of altitude to assess the signature. Instead I find myself flat on earth, feet kicking up clouds of dust, scuffing through the white powder drifts of lime that sooner or later will be thinned to nothing by the wind, washed away by the next rain, and there is always the next rain.

# GAIL TINGLE'S HORSE TROUGH

A gallon of water weighs 8.34 pounds and my horse trough—I keep it in the backyard—holds 130 gallons. As I float there in my tub—the stars floating over Winesburg—I feel—also—as if I am sinking into the wet mud below. Yes—I know about that Archimedes and the suddenness of insight—those eureka moments lapping over the lip of the floating floating vessel. Here my mind is all soggy, water-logged. And that's the way I like it. Not so much sensory deprived but depleted. I am on the edge of of of feeling, feeling feeling bleed away, unable to tell where I leave off and the water begins. Listen. Did you see that? That star peeling from the sky—falling. The nicker of gravity grabbing hold?

# THE ABANDONED FLOSS FACTORY

Once, it was a going concern, the floss factory. It employed dozens of people in Winesburg, and annually it produced many million yards of fine gauge dental floss and tape, both waxed and unwaxed varieties. The wax was procured from local beekeepers. A mint market flourished that provided the flavoring for both the floss factory and to the Wrigley gum works of Chicago. I worked summers as a child picking the mint leaves on the mint farms on the outskirts of Winesburg. I cultivated the plants as well, harrowing the white threads of the plant running from the milky tubers beneath the mulch. In the distance, I saw the three smokestacks of the floss factory emitting the braided clouds of steam. For a long time Dental Floss Days was the town's annual festival. Junior Achievement used donated seconds to manufacture string art renditions of boats or cars. We have an airplane woven out of floss above our bed. My wife flosses every night in that same bed, reading a poem while she does. I am not so diligent, and when I do floss, I do it in front of a mirror. I usually bleed a little. It is floss that comes now from China, I think, or maybe Vietnam. Someplace far away.

# JUAN REYES, LINEMAN

My father (he's gone now) was a member of the International Brotherhood of Electrical Workers as I am. One of my first memories is entering my elementary school's science fair (in kindergarten) with a project demonstrating the different circuits (series and parallel) that my father really made. My father coached me as to what to say to the judges, but I don't really remember what I said back then. Electricity is a mystery still. I like that it "flows," that it seems to know (before I would know) that the circuit is complete. It goes where it goes. I think about "the ground" a lot. Especially when I am up in the air. There is a field of utility poles I work (I don't come down often) where we string the new wire, testing the product of the Fort Wayne wire and die companies. The electricity (testy, testing) circuits aimlessly around the forest schematic, humming as it goes, snapping around the glass insulators, looking for the ground. When I buried my dad (not that far from this electric forest), I played out a lead of copper wire he held in his hand that ran to mine, not letting go as the ground was filled in around that thread. It's there still (a patinaed blade of grass), I touch when I visit, discharge (still) the sad shock of it all.

# GLORIA GLEASON'S CROCHETED PENNANTS

I hang the new ones, different colors, every day, string them up between the tulip poplar trees in the back yard. The color determines the scrub color of the day. If it is blue, the nurses and the dental hygienists will wear blue scrubs. The phlebotomist will wear blue. Anesthesiologists and X-ray technicians, blue. Even the vets, their scrubs will be blue. And not the dark blue but the powder blue, the robin's egg blue. Whatever blue I choose that day. Down at the Subs-N-You during lunch the PAs and the EMTs slouch at the tables, all blue. The colors? They just come to me. Green. The color green will come to me. I will feel the green. I will head to downtown Winesburg and Blister's Pharmacy and buy a skein or two. I'm not a knitter. I've never learned to knit. In the dusk I go out to the backyard and unravel the pennants from the branches of the trees. In the deep shadows at the borders of the yard I see the silhouettes camouflaged by the midnight blue of their scrubs color. I watch them writhe out of their clothes, emerge out of the dark in the dark, scrubbed scrubs, bleached now, bone white in the bright moonlight.

# THE DRINKING FOUNTAIN IN THROW PARK

Mother always told me to keep your mouth off the faucet. I was supposed to push the button and let the water bubble up, up over the metal nozzle, and catch it there in the air. I always thought that this was where the coldest water ever was stored. Father showed me how to run the cold water on each wrist. It was magic, he said, how the cold slap of water chilled the skin, conducted the cool through your whole body. I remember how the stones warmed up in the sun and the way the shadows of the spilled water spotting the steps disappeared as I watched. And I wasn't supposed to spit. But I did spit.

# MY GRANDFATHER'S HOG OILER

There aren't that many left. Most were gathered up during the war, scrapped for the cast iron, now probably distributed as shrapnel all over Europe and the Pacific islands. Granddad came home from that war and took the GI Bill money and put it into a farm, 80 acres, outside Winesburg. He used to say he "played" with hogs, farrowed and finished. I think I remember that place. I remember the smell that Granddad always said was, "the smell of money." The hogs were spooky. They would look at you the way a human would. And they always were escaping out of each and every more elaborate pens Granddad would, my dad would say, construct. "He was leaking pigs," dad would say. I remember visiting after the family moved to town. The yards and pens a wreck with rusting tools and implements, old seed drills and steel-wheeled harrows. There were lumps and chunks of metal the edges worn smooth where the hogs rubbed and rooted against and around them. I lugged home this souvenir, an old oiler I found mired near the busted troughs. The drums still roll and turn, but the life is all wore out of it, a curiosity, a conversation starter now I keep it in the front room. "What the hell is that?" I hope someone will say when that someone visits. But no one visits. I sit in the parlor and worry the old useless device that warms, sooner or later, to my touch.

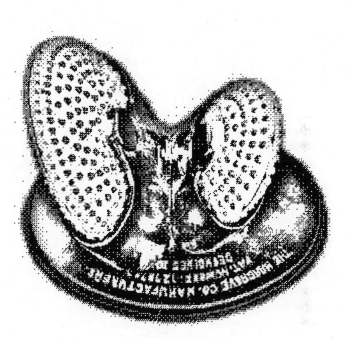

# KLAUS WEBER, CURB HOUSE NUMBERER

Around here there are no blocks as such, just cul-de-sacs and circles and dead ends and half streets and alleys. The numbers make no sense. And some of the numbers have fractions and some have letters attached as an afterthought and some have all three—numbers and fractions and letters. And the letters are upper case and lower case. The lady who lives in 2A is all the time taking mail over to 29 and vice versa. The mail trucks wander around looking for the number that might be a number. There's no rhyme or reason to it. I do use stencils so most of the job is taping the cutout paper to the curb. Then I just fill up the spaces with the aluminum paint. It glows in the light. When I finish there is this sparkling drift stuck in the gutter. And then I move on to the next house leaving the last one's number to dry. Often I am just guessing at the next number. It makes no sense as I said. Later, much later, I return to peel the stencils from the curb. Sitting there in the gutter I can't help myself. I do some weeding along the edges of the anonymous lawns. Ground mint and multi-flora rose and mimosa and crab grass. Weeds look like weeds. And they are everywhere.

# JANET VACHON'S GLIDER

I like it. They don't build them like this anymore. Nylon webbing and aluminum tubes. I had this idea that I would be one of those people who sits on an old lawn chair on her brown lawn and waves to everyone passing by. A human interest story. I pictured myself doing this. I practiced my waving. I live in the white Cape Cod with the pine green shutters the color of the webbing on my glider. I am on the side of the road, the old Lincoln Highway. Once this was the main drag. Now the only traffic are the semis avoiding the weigh station on the new US 30. There are a ton of trucks hauling caskets up from Batesville. BATESVILLE painted in gold on the sides of the black painted vans. I waved and waved. I glided and glided. And then waved some more. It got old after a while. What is a wave after all? I got to thinking it was more a gesture of surrender. "See," I would say to myself imagining I was saying it to the drivers rushing by, "Nothing up my sleeve!" Empty-handed. It isn't good to sit for that long, waving or not. They say that sitting is the new smoking. I don't know about that. But in the lulls between the casket trucks, I'd walk around. I started taking pictures of the glider with me not in it and imagined what I looked like not there from the road rushing by. What was it I was waving at? Crates filled with crates filled up with nothing. And were those waves I was giving away for free, were they an expression of fare thee well? Or comeback comeback. Wait, wait for me?

# GARY FRANKE'S FAN

I inherited it from my dad who died last summer. I grew up with this fan that was stationed in the window of the converted attic bedroom where I slept, the Clover Lane house in Winesburg. It was hot in the summers in that room at night. The ceiling there sloped to floor, the underside of the roof, baking all day. Dad rigged the fan so it would draw the hot air out the window. He would patiently explain his thinking on the thermal dynamics as he tied the handle of the fan to the handle of the window frame with a leftover extension cord. It didn't make sense to me then, and, to tell you the truth, it doesn't make sense to me now. I wanted the outside air to be blown into the room, and I would stay up late into the night dismantling the fan's arrangement, reinstalling it, reversing the draw. I would wake up early the next morning and reverse the fan again, back to Dad's original configuration. That's how old I am. It was an old fan. All metal and not equipped with a switch to switch the directions of the blades to draw or to blow. Now, I have air-conditioning, whole house. I keep the fan on the floor like a panting pet. I leave it on all day, all night, murmuring in the corner. It moves the air around in this room. It stirs and drafts. My dad is all wound up in that machine. I turn it toward me, the air spilling my way. I turn it away and feel nothing.

# THE DEAD MALL

I still broadcast my cable show from the deserted and ruined food court. Yesterday, I talked with Beth Ehler, a nurse, who gave me a quadrivalent flu shot on air. I own a one-person advertising shop, doing coupons, mainly, for the Stetler's Auto Parts. Years ago, I had the idea of doing this PSA filled infomercial each noon on WEEP-TV in Winesburg. The wicker chairs and wicker screens, the ferns and the mother-in-law tongues were my idea. They are with me still though the wicker is worse for wear and the plants need dusting. Once, we had an audience applauding between bites of the pizza slices and chop suey. Back then I worried that the bells and buzzers from the arcade would drown out the audio track. There was a shoe store over there, and you could watch people try on shoes in the background of so many episodes. I thought of them as the show's dancers, my chorus line. At night, I watch the tapes. I still have tapes. And I can track the dwindling. There I am talking talking talking talking. Middle school kids are singing. Karate classes are kicking. The Kiwanis are raising money. This dog, this cat needs adopting. And the set grows dimmer. And the ambient noise hushes up. The wicker frays. And more likely than not I am there alone on the little stage, no one to interview, no one anymore urgently seeking access to public access TV. One day, you look up and you realize you are this hermit in a ruin. I swear I must feel like that Roman centuries ago walking the streets of Rome thinking he is still a citizen of a vast empire when he notices, suddenly, the walls of the grand coliseum are being quarried by the Visigoths to build their outhouses and the center of the world he thought he once inhabited is now smack dab in the middle of nowhere.

# THE WINESBURG MOIST TOWELETTE COMPANY

In the spring, the Winesburg Moist Towelette Company holds an open house. Tours are given of the facility. All the machinery and most of the employees reek of the lemon scent that is a proprietary trademark odor of the company. Even the company's one forklift, as it shuttles and scuttles over the floor, leaves in its wake a citrusy aroma. Everything seems very hygienic of course. The alcohol is kept in gleaming steel vats. You have to wear hairnets and tissue booties over your shoes. You are told that the tissue booties that you wear over your shoes are made in a factory up in South Bend, and you get to keep them after the open house is over. I have several pairs in the downstairs closet by the door. There is a demonstration of how to fold the soaked paper into smaller and smaller squares so that, in the end, it fits inside the wrapping neatly. That's where the money is, you're told, in the advertisements and the logos printed on the wrapper. You get to take one or two when you exit the open house. They tell you about the shelf life. I like to tear into mine soon, the next week, after the open house closes down, knowing I can get another pack a year from now. I like that little burst of lemon that escapes, and how it excites the memory of the day over not too long ago. I like, too, the feel of the alcohol, how it cools the skin as it evaporates, molecule by molecule, into the Indiana air, and I like to see the careful creases disappear, another magical disappearance, a lingering loss.

# FOUND IN GABRIEL WICHERN'S BACKYARD

It is as close as we get to a real ruin round here, a giant cement arrow in the backyard pointing east, pointing (we figure) toward Fort Wayne. We figure further that it must have been some kind of aid to navigation for ancient airplanes and airships plying the skies over Winesburg a century ago. The old mail routes maybe. If you look closely you can see indications of paint, a white wash all washed out with age. The concrete's now cracked and crazed, heaves from a bunch of frosts and thaws. It must have been some important news that needed sent by what would have been new-fangled technologies to move that mail. But maybe it was just the mundane messages of yesterday's weather or Sunday's meal that someone sprung an extra penny or two to expedite cross-country. Back then there must have been a ton of wrecks, airplanes falling from the sky, lost in darkness, in fog, in snow. A neighbor will report while spading a garden that a warped bicycle-spoked landing gear will turn up in the dirt. Or after a hard rain an old brass compass or altimeter will percolate up through the mud. More ruin. I like to sit on the crumbling pad and face east, following the direction of the direction, watching the evening come, rising from the general vicinity of Fort Wayne. Really, I swear, I've got nothing better to do.

69

# GRANT STACEY'S VAC-U-FORM

It could never be sold today. Too dangerous. Mattel got away with murder in the 60's, this oven that melted sheets of plastic soft enough to be shaped over a mold, the vacuum pump sucking the air away and fusing the hardening plastic back into the desired shape. I love the smell of that plastic on the edge of burning. You probe it in its frame over the oven as it heats. I use the eraser end of a pencil, punching the corners, drumming the center to the point that it just gives, is pliable enough just right before, a moment or two, it would begin to melt through. There's then the swing of the whole framed contraption over to the perforated table where the mold's been fixed and then the pumping that handle like the devil and then the miraculous shaping of the thing out of nothing but the gulping slurp of air. And there you have it—a cheap trinket or charm. It is so dangerous. The heating element is out in the open, not shielded in any way. I keep it down in the basement, behind locked doors, away from the kids who stand outside and listen as I pump the air out from underneath an afterthought and smell burning plastic or singed air.

# CLAYTON TANG, BUSINESS SIGN PAINTER

I used to paint signs, hand-painted paint on the plate glass of stores in the downtown business district of Winesburg. I specialized in a cursive script, eschewing the block letter printing. I excelled at serifs. I was a master with mahl sticks. I moved from window to window, painting "SALE" in my sleep through the calendar of minor holidays—Presidents' Birthdays, Labor Days, Columbus Days. I loved ellipses, eyeballing the distance between the dots, the periods of periods . . . But that all changed with the melting of the economy. There was plenty of work as business decelerated and shrank. Have you heard that glass is not quite a solid, that it flows on some far edge of liquid so that old panes reveal a thickening at the bottom as the invisible viscous nature settles out like the air leaking out of the whole enterprising enterprise. Now, I stay busy whitewashing the insides of the soon-to-be-abandoned storefronts, sketching out the "GOING OUT OF BUSINESS" sign in a defeated freehand and then painting over even that, a cloudy post-literate alphabet of forgetting, an impressionistic amnesiac smear.

# THE CITY MANAGER: ATTRACTIVE NUISANCE PARK

One of the several neighborhood "vest pocket" playgrounds administered by the Winesburg Park Board, the Attractive Nuisance Park has several enticing hazards and come-hither obstacles, including a four cord climbing structure scattered on a muddy hillside. The park has been closed since 1996, the court case still wending its way through the appellate process. The park is enclosed by a rusting cyclone fence that is inexplicably topped by neon lighting and is itself enclosed by a superstructure of scaffolding and rope netting and posted with numerous posters and placards warning of dangers in a variety of illegible scripts.

# BACK TO SCHOOL AT THE WINESBURG SCHOOL OF CHIROPRACTIC

First opening its doors in 1948, WSC readies itself for a new class perspective practitioners of the art of chiropractic manipulation. I love the smell of students in the fall. A joke, I joke. I have been here from the start, using my GI Bill money to attend the Palmer College of Chiropractic in Davenport. It was my idea to purchase the surplus Quonset hut to stand for our clinic. I thought it would be a kind of architectural "duck," a building that advertises, via its shape and structure, the product it houses. Here, a limberness and pliant roofline, the wall, solidly planted on a grounded foundation, turning into a roof and then back into the wall again. Vaulted, almost cathedral-like. Seamless. I like to greet the students at the door. "You've brought your backs back to school," I joke. It's a quip I heard long ago in the Quad Cities. And every fall, I recall that most fortunate matriculation. There I donned the white coat, and from the bluff by Old Palmer, I looked over the spine of the old river flowing under the arches, the suspension cables, the trusses stitched with that nervous energy of transport. Bridge after bridge after bridge after bridge.

# ERNESTINA STEVENS, HYDROLOGIST POET

They stopped making most of the jars down in Muncie a while ago, but the Ball people kept open a little living history boutique factory where they blow these blue afterthoughts and sell them as souvenirs. I fetch them back to Winesburg in six-packs. I was trained as a hydrologist and came here to collect data on leeching, seeping, and percolating water around here. I wrote the book on the manner in which the Fork River disappears underground, eroding, dissolving as it does the limestone underlayment. But that was years ago, years that have all washed away. Now, I am retired and so I travel a bit, go where the winds take me. There and there I collect the rainwater in blue Ball jars and bring them back to this town. The samples fill up the jars at different levels, and, I imagine refract the blue sunlight in solution in each jar. I place them here and there all over town, in groups sometime, more often all by their lonesome. The jars look good nesting in the green uncut grass, catching the rhyming light sifting through the constant clouds, and then letting it go.

# THE WINESBURG Y

For all I know, I am the last resident of a YMCA, a YMCA anywhere. The Winesburg Y has this one room left on the second floor over the cardio studio below. The other dorm rooms have been converted for yoga or step. The whole wall is mirrored. Over the years, the other residents in those other rooms drifted away, disappeared, skipped without paying the rate. It dwindled down to me. Years ago I realized that the management no matter how much they wanted me out wouldn't do anything to hasten my departure as long as I paid the rent. They are Christian after all. We are all waiting for me to pass. I kind of haunt the place. I have been asked not to scare the children, stay out of sight during the life saving classes. I have to smoke outdoors several hundred feet from the entrance. After hours, I make a little extra change washing and drying the workout towels. I roll them into rolls and stack them into furry pyramids on the check-in desk. The building, at night, when I am left alone in it after hours, is pretty quiet. It has settled. No creaks or pops. I like to turn on the treadmills, all six of them, set them on different speeds, let them run the sixty minutes limit. I listen to the hum seep up through the floor—the acoustic ceiling tiles have long lost their dampening qualities, waterlogged with leaks, broken, rotten, sifting into dust. It is a kind of lullaby. I am asleep before the pulse of the belt runs out.

# CLAUDE BURKE, SWAN BOATING ON THE FORK RIVER

I find it very relaxing. You rent the boats by the hour. I find I drift along for hours. I don't even pump the pedals to turn the paddles. I like the deep base thump when the wave wake of a passing Ski-Doo slaps the fiberglass hull. It relaxes me. I am retired and this is retiring. My game was insurance. Well, not insurance exactly but reinsurance. I insured insurance. It's the way insurance companies lay off the bet on this or that mortality. I worked for the Lincoln Life in Fort Wayne, and there I relaxed in the museum. I liked looking at the daguerreotypes of President Lincoln they have there. What were the odds that he would have ended up the way he did? You know you never step into the same river twice. What were the odds when I was looking at all those cracked faces on all that cracked glass, that I would end up floating, circling slowly, stuffed in this blanched goose, rudderless, on a river, a lost river, that somewhere around here disappears through a fissure into whatever the hell is underground.

# TECHNIQUES FOR PAINTING EYES

I have been in this basement since junior high school painting 54mm military miniatures. If you are going to take up this hobby you are probably going to do soldiers from the Napoleonic Wars. The uniforms (and the whole point of this is researching and painting accurate uniforms) are the best. Just all the different blues—Russian, Prussian, French, Polish. All the regiments. The different hats of the cavalry—shakos, busbies, kepis. The braid alone. The piping and darting. The wrinkles in all the lead turned into soft cloth by chiaroscuro. But the eyes are the hardest. The eyes take the most time. I like to start with the big white splotch and then whittle away at that splat, shaping it into that almond shape by nudging the lids nearer, nearer. But the eyes are hard because you are staring with all your eyes at these eyes you're making. And you are seeing the eyes through all the lenses and loops you have fixed to magnify the eye, the head the size of a pea, dabbing at pixels with the 000 sable brush. I do lick the tip of the brush, the one or two hairs, into the finest point for the iris, the pupil. In the basement, with my eye, not blinking, screwed down to see the eye I am painting become like the eye that is seeing the eye, the layers of enamel, stain, wash, the transparent pentimento, that flicker of sight, the dot of white on white that is a reflection of a reflection caught there in what could be called the corner of the eye.

# JERSEY BERM SELF-STORAGE

It isn't like we actually build new roads or even improve the roads we have here in Winesburg. But we do have a lot of berms. We keep them in a lot out by the eraser factory. Come to think of it, they do look something like outsized erasers stacked like that. We wait for a highway appropriation to come through or, at the very least, a notice by the Department of Homeland Security that something around here has been designated a target that it is under some kind of threat. The berms then can deter. They can baffle. They can screen, offering protection against attack. Every berm has been adopted by someone here in town. Adopt-a-berm. Or two. I have four actually. My idea is to all get together and make one giant maze, a maze or a labyrinth. I have forgotten now what the difference is. All I know is that it would take up a lot of time. The building of it. And the getting lost deep inside it.

# PATTY PANE, HORTICULTURALIST

Everywhere I can start a start I do. Here in Winesburg, we live in the lee of the lake, the lake that generates the lake effect—snow in the winter but mostly hedgerows of clouds every season. The sunlight just isn't available to us here. We search for our shadows on the gloomy ground. So I like to put out feelers, cultivate every inch of the gloaming. Start my start. I like to watch the leaves lick the meager photons from the sky, lap up the half-baked loaves of illumination. The heart-shaped leaves, tropic, twist and turn, palpitating, palpate, slaphappy. All the jelly I had to eat to empty all the jars of jelly. Standing at the window, sucking on a spoon, I look out through the green curtain and watch the sun set somewhere out there, sinking through the sodden clouds.

# GENE SELMER AND THE BAND INSTRUMENT LYRE TEST TRACK

Conn up in Elkhart makes the marching band instruments, but here I make the little lyres that hold the flip-books or music. Out back I have a little test track. I have all the instruments, all the different sizes and shapes of brass and reed. I am not a very good player, but I can pass. I have the music for "Horse" for all the parts. I never really understood why the music holder had to look like a musical instrument. Why does the lyre look like a lyre? It's like those pilot fishes attached to the shark. I have a lyre too. I march around the track striking the tuned metal bars, making a sound like horseshoes prancing on plumbing going through the paces of "Horse." The lyre has a lyre. It works pretty well considering it is a percussion instrument. It's me, the reason why Winesburg has this crinkly sound in the dusk, me testing the lyres. That and the inordinate number of wind chimes that are never in tune, scattered around the town.

# SHAUN DOWNY'S FEAR

I'm fine with regular ladders, extension ladders if you will. The ladders that you lean against the thing you are climbing up—the house, the wall—the ones with rungs. Step ladders, I can tolerate, but only the tall ones, the ones with four or more steps and the hinged ledge you flip out near the top to rest a paint bucket on. It is the small stepladders, the squat ones they also call the step stool, that makes me feel uncomfortable. I suffer a kind of reverse vertigo, a syncope that hugs the ground. I look and look at these stout contraptions and they don't make sense to me. They seem so, I don't know, noncommittal to the going up, sunk and countersunk, sinking into the floor below. Here, we have the tip of the step iceberg not for climbing up but for climbing down. It's a matter of gravity, the grave center of gravity, gravity folding in on itself. The weight waiting like that.

# DICK THOMAS, RETIRED SALESMAN

I worked for Wrigley's up in Chicago for thirty years. My territory was northeastern Indiana. You would not believe the number of places that carried gum. I pushed product, stocked shelves. I couldn't park the car, a company car, in the garage because it was packed to the gills with gum. My boys, Brad and Rick, would break into the inventory and handout packs to all the neighborhood kids. I'd find the red plastic strings that opened the packs, the dusty silver inner wrapper, the paper sleeves all over the lawn. Double-Mint. I seem to remember everyone I met was chewing chewing gum back then. It is all nervous energy. An elaborate method of worry. Now that I am retired, I like to walk up and down downtown. I watch where I step. An old habit. The streets of Winesburg are paved with gum, the sidewalks blistered over, a rash, a sticky braille. I fancy myself an archeologist of a sort, on my hands and knees with dental instruments excavating the black mastic layers of the past's mastication. The flavor's spent, ground down into a fossil record of time's teeth grinding. As telling as dentition, the petrified impression of a molar is imprinted there and there and there again and again and again from eons ago.

# FIELD TESTING FOOT MEASURING DEVICES

Winesburg has been designated a regional center for assessing the accuracy of experimental Brannock Devices in real world situations and simulations. I had been in the shoe business for years and then one day I realized I wasn't so much in the shoe business but the foot business. It was a better fit for me. I am most interested in the issues of expansion and contraction. Expansion and contraction of both the biological foot and the alloys that make up the Device's metallic superstructure. Certain atmospheric conditions can affect the metrics of the instrument beyond the approved tolerances dictated by the Department of Health and Human Services. The humidity of the region, the heat, perhaps, even the gravitational fields here influence the swelling and shrinking of the feet under scrutiny. I am pretty sure I can see such movement happening before my eyes, measured by the various scales and slides of the device. But to tell you the truth, a foot in my hand, any foot now after all these years, the heft of it, its topography under my touch, a fit like a glove.

# FRED BURKE, NAME TAG RECYCLER

I hang out after receptions, conventions, any gathering where adhesive nametags are used. I try to make myself look official at the doorway and ask for the nametags from people as they leave. Because they are wearing nametags with names written in the white space below the printed message—Hello, my name is—I know their name. "Hello, Jim," I will say, "let me take that for you." And proceed to peel the labels from their lapels. I bring a sheet of empty backing and reapply the adhesive side to the shiny paper. Once I get the now filled-up sheets back to the shop, I take the white out out and coat the Sharpie-shaped lettering and blot the names out, feathering the fluid to blend into the unmarked whiteness of the space. You can't even tell the name was ever there. I introduce an element of the unknown again, a liquid forgetfulness that hardens into a solid blank slate. You can say I reintroduce possibilities. Everything is once again up for grabs. Hello, Hello!

# CAPTAIN SKIP HEDWHIG, DRUG DUSTER

I don't work for Lilly. I contract out my services. Have been up here for years. Aerial application such as this is most often associated with agriculture, a plant thing. The first time anybody attempted it was 100 years ago right next door in Ohio where they sprayed bag worms on catalpa trees with an aerosol of arsenic and lead. We, the crop dusting community, didn't look back. We've expanded actually. You will find us taking wing up over the desperate little cities of the flyover. Here I am applying the etherized version of a selective serotonin reuptake inhibitor. That's right, an SSRI. I like the initials. Their sound mimics the sizzling roar of my craft. I like to sortie on a gray day, the lake effect overcast bearing down on Winesburg. I like to believe that the cargo I deliver turns that brooding sky blue. Not the blue of the blues, you understand, but that other, bluey blue blue.

# MAURICE MILKIN, ERASER CARVER

I go to the Pink Pearl factory store at the factory and buy the ones, discounted, beyond their expiration date. Stale erasers. I have been sculpting for years. Sculpting is about seeing what is not there, the negative space, the foil, the relief. It isn't lost upon me that in my way I am erasing the eraser, whittling it away one rubber sliver at a time. In the end I have a rubber stamp embossed with a word. I use the stamp to stamp. I have a stamp that stamps STAMP. I have turned these erasers of flat language, turned them into these words with enough depth, a lip. It's a slug of spongy type. I tool these one-word stories, use blue impermeable ink. MOM for instance. DAD. GRAM. YOU. DEAR. LOST. GONE. ?.

# FOR SALE. BABY SHOES. NO LONGER WORN.

And they are bronzed. I found them in the front yard
when I was tearing out the lawn to do some midwestern xeriscaping. The bronzed shoes were like a reef, a
drift, a shoal of shoes just below the sod. One emerged
then clumps of two, three scalloped together. All different
kinds. Saddle oxfords, slip-ons, loafers, mocs. I liked the
ways the laces were frozen into knots or not but fossilized
into limping coils and frayed braids. I polished them up.
They took on that burnished light, a tanned tarnish. Can
I interest you in a shoe? Or two? Who knows what else
is buried here underground. I have a lot more lawn to go.
And what with all the freezes and thaws, we will all be
surprised what that yard, all pea gravel and chipped wood
in the very near future, will heave up into the dying light.

# THE HISTORICALLY PRESERVED TELEPHONE BOOTH OF WINESBURG, INDIANA

When you close the door, you don't know this, you can close the door and when you close the door, the doors really, they are a kind of folding, scissoring kind of door, when you close them a light in the ceiling comes on. It might be a fluorescent, but I don't think so. I think it is an old-fashioned incandescent bulb there behind a yellowing plastic globe. And when the light comes on you can see the sediment of dead insects, hundreds of them layering the bottom hemisphere of the stained globe. Moths and flies attracted to the light, I guess, the heat, getting caught inside the globe's baffle, baffled and beaten up in there, finally, by the beating up against the flickering light. Winesburg just never took the phone booth away. As if we forgot it was there. It is a registered historical building now, even the dead bugs are historical. Public hearings would have to be held to remove them. Days go by, that's what history is, and the phone will ring, that is to say, the phone will make a ringing sound, a ring will be generated from somewhere inside the old and getting older telephone. And the collectors who collect those kinds of things, who are waiting there by the phone booth day and night for just such an occasion, will turn on their antique tape recorders attempting to capture the ancient mechanical peal of the artifact, actually rearranging the molecules jostling on the magnetic tape spooling through their own sad and obsolete machines.

# ZEKE REMKE, FISHING LURE MAKER

I think I might be the last, the last of the lure makers. There was a time when there were hundreds of lure makers, reel manufacturers, line weavers, tackle factories of all kinds within a fifty mile radius of Fort Wayne. It is the lakes, the hundreds of lakes with all the fish in all the lakes of northeastern Indiana. Henry Dills, a conductor on the B&O up in Garrett, whittled the first lure, a wiggler, out of local cedar in his caboose. He founded the Creek Chub Bait Company, and the rest of us just chased after him. I am the last as I said. No one fishes anymore with these lunks of wood, these painted splinters. With me gone, all the techniques will be lost like the way you get the scaling of the scales. Hint: it is a wedding veil, the best stencil ever. This once was the leading edge of the technology. Innovators, all of them who thought like the perch and sunfish, the pike and cat. My specialty is the wounded minnow, but I love to thread together the endless segments of the baby eel. The largest large mouth bass ever hooked was lured by an Indiana lure. I go over to Lake Wawasee and stand on the marina dock, covered with my lures, hooked into every inch of my clothes. I am a walking display, a lure myself. Who will take the bait? Buy one of the spoons or spinners? You don't even have to fish with it, but put it in a frame and display it as a strange object of beauty.

# JUANITA'S QUICK NAILS

Here's a list of names of shades popular now in Winesburg: "Plenty of Fish in the Sea," "Keep it Up," "Jaded," "Jailbait," "Lonesome Dove," "Eternal Pessimist," "Black Star," "Gray Area," "Thanks a Latte," "My Silicone Popped," "Ants in My Pants," "Gone Gray," "Wine Not," "Mr. Sandman," "My Button Fell Off," and "I Only Eat Salads." There are a lot of blues, inky colors, blacks. I like the lacquers with that deep gloss polish. I can see myself in the deep pool of blue, a thumbnail picture of me so to speak, bent to this work. I can read the life in the cuticle, the brittle keratin, the nicks and nibbles on the nail. Forget the palms. It's all in the nails. And it's not pretty.

# THE CANOLA FIELD WEST OF WINESBURG

You look twice, maybe even twice more, that field taken by all that yellow. You think it must be weeds or mustard. But it is Canola. Rapeseed really. The Canadians renamed it—CANada Oil. But the new name makes you think of crayons, Crayola. And it's the color, a cartoon. A smear that smudges out the outlines of the routine greens of the ancient corn and bean fields hereabouts. The yellow, every year, expands. It is a soothing color you guess, a dangerous safety yellow that paints the insides of your eyelids if you look at it too long, an after-image of a camera's flash, stabbing. You are yoked to this yolk.

# SUE JOHNSON, PARKING ENFORCEMENT OFFICER

I have one of those new digital wearable fitness devices that counts the number of steps I take each day. If you aren't moving enough there is a tiny picture on the tiny screen, a frowning face. If you are moving the face changes to a smile that gets bigger and bigger as you take more and more steps. That's all I do is walk. I chalk parked car tires, circling the downtown parking spaces of Winesburg every two hours. That's all you get of free parking, two hours. I time my walks. I have been doing this long enough I can mark the time by the number of steps I take. The marks I make with the chalk look like smiles too, smack dab on the treads of the driver's side rear tire. Tire after tire. Two hours later, my pedometer smiling its biggest smile, I come back around. I mark the more recent parked cars, the tires a blank slate. But then there are the ones with the telltale mark from two hours before. I have to write them up. I can do that while I am walking, writing up the summons as I circle the infracting vehicle. I leave the ticket under the windshield wiper blade as I march in place. You can say I am motivated to move even as I enforce the sustained periods of standing still.

# SIGRID STARR, SERVER, THE HUDDLE HOUSE

It is either the last thing I do at night or the first thing I do in the morning. I am no longer sure as The Huddle stays open all night and every day all the time. I gather all the ketchup bottles together, a bottle round up, and ascertain the bottles that are half full or half empty. Let me say first, there is a lot of call for ketchup at The Huddle House. It seems its customers like to employ the condiment on about everything. I like mine on the potatoes. But many people like to inject their scrambled eggs with the ketchup, scrambling them even more as they work in the dressing. But where was I? Yes, the bottles and the procedure of using up the dregs of one bottle to top off the contents of another. Sometimes, I can have a dozen or so mating pairs operating at any one time. Time. There is a time, that time at night when time itself is thrown out of whack. Three, four in the morning, the components of time forget how long or short their duration. The ketchup, gravity's stooge, decides at last to slide through the bottlenecks, a red inertia. You know ketchup is a colloidal suspension. You don't need to rap it on the bottom to get things started. A thump on the side works just as well. But the herd of kissing bottles late at night, early in the morning find a way to find their levels, hourglasses that take hours to right themselves.

# JUNIOR LEAGUE GIFT WRAPPING TABLE

We started, when?, during the Christmas holiday maybe twenty years ago. That Christmas came and went. And, well, we just stayed open, wrapping. And the people of Winesburg seemed to have had a lot of things they needed to have wrapped. We can't list here everything we've wrapped. It might be easier to say what we haven't wrapped. Though to tell you the truth nothing comes to mind. We have wrapped things that we had already wrapped. We'd say, "We recognize that wrapping." We have developed a certain style. And the paper? We have had a preference for certain patterns over the years. Colors. Textures. We arrive at the table to find, every day, a queue, a few people deep, their arms filled with this and that all wanting them to be wrapped. It's become, over the years, more a ritual, a rite, or maybe a kind of therapy. We make clear which is the outside, which is in. We stately measure. Measure twice, three or more times. Cut once. We really *look* at the object to be wrapped. We are good thinking spatially, can hold it in our heads, all the dimensions of all the things to be wrapped, even time. For us, we cover every nook and cranny of every surface with a new surface as if we have turned everything's insides out.

# SANDRA AND CINDY POPP, ZOOMERS

Inspired by the movie *Powers of Ten*, written and directed by Charles and Ray Eames, Sandra, assisted by her husband Wilmore Popp, zooms around her Winesburg backyard in the bucket of a surplus I&M boom truck, taking pictures of herself, in the bucket of the boom truck, reflected in a mirror salvaged from the Broken Mirror Boutique. It is a two-way mirror as well and on its other side her twin sister Cindy Popp assisted by her husband Gaylord, Wilmore's brother, also riding in a bucket of a boom truck, swoops in and out of focus, approaching and retreating from the glass, recording her sister swooping, going in and out of focus on the other side. The hydraulics of the two boom trucks hum and stutter, sneeze and hiss as the sisters swing and swirl, their cameras tsking and lisping. After the day's session, the sisters download their images of each other. They watch themselves shrink and expand, stretch and collapse, the reflections of each other telescoping, scalloping, scaling up and down, exploding into clouds of duplicated pixels doubled, collaged.

# THE DOPPLER EFFECT RESEARCH STATION

Maintained by the National Oceanic and Atmospheric Administration (NOAA), the station's siren's test bed array emits variously pitched and periodic sonic events pretty much continuously to ascertain the veracity of Doppler's description of the changes in frequency of a wave for an observer moving relative to its source. In the spring, the station records the faint warbling generated by the tire tests at the Indianapolis 500 in Speedway over 100 miles to the south, amplifies them, and returns echoing reverberations. Most sounds are produced either above or below the thresholds registered by human hearing, creating in the populace all around a certain unmeasurable anxiety.

# GRAHAM WALTER'S FIGHTING KITES ARE FIGHTING

I am the only one I know in town who has kites, fighting kites, and am looking to fight them. They're Afghan kites. I use the traditional Manjha cured with a special mix of glue and ground glass. It's a panda weave of nine cotton threads, a cotton line coated with Manjha, my favorite. I like these kites, designed as they are to be unstable, on the edge always of falling out of flying. Only there at the limits of physics can you find the room to make up maneuvers to move. The kites seem spastic, spinning, jinking, juking. The sky over Winesburg is so big and so empty. My kites—I have a reel on each hand—are black commas cutting and hovering, diving and climbing on the blued sky, angry accents, ampersands. Periods period. My left hand doesn't know what the right is doing and vice versa.

# ALEXANDRIA FLOWERS TAKES HER LIMBIC SYSTEM FOR A WALK

Most evenings she exercises her emotions, strolling the side streets of Winesburg, allowing the complex set of brain structures netting up the thalamus to process the countless stimulations received that day. She has taken to drinking a dram of aquavit in which a pinch of gold salts is dissolved before her perambulation. She believes the precious metal accumulates there in the seat of emotion, gilding each synaptic gap, plating the receptors with a highly conductive paste. She feels she feels things. She feels even her feelings have feelings. As the day deconstructs itself all around her, her paleomammalian brain dismantles the filters of sensation she deploys to distinguish (a kind of panning in a stream) the nugget in the dross. Everything, in the gloaming, becomes gold. Everything becomes *the* (italics added by her) thing.

# SUSAN APP, TRUANCY SECRETARY

All day, I make the calls. I check on absences. The rolls come in from the homerooms right after the first bell, collected by dedicated student-aids, circulating through the contagious corridors and hallways. The stairwell sings and sewers. Names of the absent. The never-made-it-in. I contact the contact numbers. I push the number buttons with the eraser on my pencil. No one is home. No one is ever home. Or, no, I imagine them at home in bed, the situation dire. So sick, so smitten that no one can reach the jangling phone on the table next to the sick bed. It rings and rings. Sometime there are ghostly recordings, ghosts in the machine. "We can't make it to the phone right now . . ." I see them wasting away, sweaty in soiled sheets. The stench. The pestilence. Chronic illness is chronic. I put a check mark next to the names, a vector indicating that I will call them back. I call them back. I call them back. Receive the stutter of the persistent ring. Percussive pertussis. A buzz like a biting sting. Allergic to my ear. I am, sad to say, the only one who will receive, in the next hopeful spring, a certificate, I will make myself, recognizing perfect perfect attendance.

# THE CANTOR QUADRUPLETS

The town donated a house to us. It came with a town-do-
nated trailer out back, back in the corner of the lot, its
tires shot, hitch rusted out, propane cans empty empty.
The used trailer was another donation to us, to the local miracle of us, along with a lifetime supply of diapers,
another lifetime supply of formula, another lifetime supply of car seats, and a gross of pacifiers. We thought our
folks thought that, one day, fixed up, we'd all haul the
whole wreck over some horizon, the hole wreck of us,
get the smell out of Dodge at least for a weak-end. Go
to *The Lake*. Skate. Rent space in the gravelscape of an
overgrown KIA. Any place other than the here-and-now
that more-and-more was looking like the here-and-ever-
after-after. After the old man split for some greener pas-
tures, Mom, she started holing up in that tin can. "Me
time," she called it. "You kids," she'd swell, "stay in the
goddamn yard." She drank Cutty Dixie cups, fond, she
was, of the green bottle's picture, a sad ship reaching on
some tactless tack, and sift through slick magazines and
the old joyless *Joy of Looking*, ripping out pages of rec-
ipes for stews and ragouts she never made, finding the
fine print too fine. Starting. Starting lists. Starting lists of
ingredients. We ate out of cans. We saw her through the
hatches and holes as we ran past, red-rovering, crack-the-
whipping, staying staying in the yard. At night, no light.
We hunted down lumbering lightning bugs, crushed them
out like cigarettes in our palms, their butt ash throbbing
the there there there there. In that dark, she trailed out of
the trailer, climbed the latter to the heap's hump roof like
she was climbing out of under underwater and floated on
the surface of a silver pool and Mom mom-bathed in the
mooning moonlight, one big refracting reflection, shadows bouncing around, dodge balls getting out of Dodge.

The yard shingled with the shells of sucked dry pet milk cans breeched with the beak of a chirp key, and all of us us-es, staying in the goddamn yard, staying frozen in this freeze tag 'til this lifetime supply of Hell's Hell freezes over.

# GLYNIS SMART'S WOODEN ICE CREAM SPOON

We found it in her things after she died. We were preparing for the estate sale. She kept it in a milk glass bowl on the marble windowsill over the kitchen sink next to the jelly glass with what was left of a wilting potato start. She did love herself some ice cream and preferred, she always said, a flat wooden spoon. A metal utensil set up a circuit, she contended, wired the bridgework and the general dentistry of her mouth into a series of dull exquisite headaches. I think she liked the taste too, the under note of cellulose ribboned into the frozen dessert. We found other spoons still in their paper sleeves, but she seemed to prefer this one spoon, broken in over all those evenings of chiseling into single serving Dixie cups on her front porch. What price do we put upon this? The milk glass is attractive enough. There is some value there. But the spoon, this little splinter, we worry it. It is a shaving, planed and plain. Don't tell anyone. I will probably pocket it. Keep it in my pocket. This relic. This bit. Handled. Kissed.

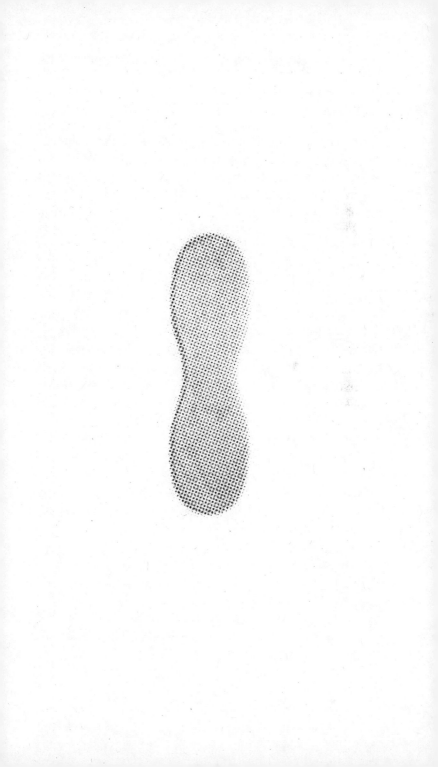

# THE CITY MANAGER: FELICITY GRAHAM'S STEREOPTICON CARD COLLECTION

She has hundreds of them, the cards with the two slightly out of sync photographs many of them hand-colored. Her collection focuses on cards that depict camera obscura of the 19th century, celestial observatories, oculara, panorama of the Grand Canyon, Fresnel lenses of lighthouses, and Civil War Cyclorama. Nightly, she has the neighbors over. They amuse themselves optically with the illusion of depth generated by the apparatus in the vitreous gel of their eyeballs. They document the history of vision, see seeing or, more exactly, they catalog all the ways the eye is tricked so easily. They peer into the shielded scope of the device, lose themselves in the steeplechase of sight, tripping over the layers of depth that forced perspective forces, the distortion more pleasing than the twilit vista of some indeterminate vanishing point plastered there somewhere out the apparently transparent windows.

# LESLIE SANGUINE, CAFETERIA CASHIER

I believe everyone in the school, including the teachers,
receive a free or reduced lunch. I am for show, running
the old mechanical NCR register, registering the chits
ringing up the dimes. Afterwards, I wipe the tables down,
restore the order to the condiments, turning the catsup
bottles into hourglasses, dripping what's left of one bottle into the leavings of the other. Gravity works, okay?
I sweep up the litter of each day's notes that the kids'
mom's have packed with their cold lunches, little scraps
of paper with messages, instructions, prayers. Half-baked
home-baked sentiments, fortune cookie scribbles slipped
in the pails and sacks. "Try to have a good enough day,
Tim!" "Don't fret too much!" "Hope you do a better
job in math." "Don't embarrass yourself or us!!!" That
kind of thing. Or sometimes just a penciled face. One big
O with three little o's inside. Oh, oh, oh, oh. My other
job—we all work other jobs—is restocking the greeting
cards concessions in town. The rack at Blister's Pharmacy
downtown. Rumi's Cigar Store. Rupp and Otting's Market, the Five and Dime, the news stand in the courthouse
run by the blind. I've noticed that the birthday cards, the
ones for weddings, new births, anniversaries languish
while the get-well ones and the cards of sympathy and
bereavement fly out the doors. I work on commission.
Pennies a card. After hours, on my hands and knees, I
count out from the cartons the somber cards and their
dour envelopes and count them into their predetermined
slots of the racks. It is like another cafeteria line. Not
quite free or reduced grief. When you care enough to send
the very best. Here you go. All you can eat. One more
fresh smorgasbord of sad sadnesses.

107

# HOWARD JUNKER, FACILITIES ENGINEER

My friends call me "How." "How, how you do this?" I get asked all the time. I always know how. How to tape and mud the drywall. How to build a header and shim a door frame. How to wire and plumb. How to snap a line. How to fire the boilers, move the steam. How to make all the clocks run on time. My workshop is a shack I built on the roof I roofed. There on the Masonite top of my workbench all the guts of the appliances are spread. I built them from scratch. My tools, a silver and steel Milky Way on pegboard overhead. Coffee cans of fasteners. Tupperware tubs of fuses, switches, drawer pulls. I know how to maintain. I know how to maintain. Look! Do you hear that? This mechanical calculator I salvaged from Mr. Rice's physics lab thirty years ago is still running. Big as a breadbox, studded and stuttering with gears and ratchets and armatures and levers, it has been sawing away all that time. Long ago, I told the machine to perform an impossible task. I divided a whole number by 0 and the contraption's workings have been searching all this time (in the toothed flanges, greased widgets, stripped screws) for the mechanical expression of infinity. The machine makes a racket as it calibrates, clucking and clunking, at any moment on the edge of inertia, unengineering itself, a twitching pile of junk. But it goes on and on. How does it do it? I maintain it. I tend to it. It will keep looking for infinity forever. It is a little engine that asks how how how how. How's time machine telling time.

# THE CITY MANAGER: WINESBURG'S ZEN GARDEN

A gift from the people of Takaoka, Japan (a suburb of Hiroshima), Winesburg's sister city, the garden is sited in the parking lot of the derelict Glenglen Mall. The garden uses lost and unclaimed luggage in place of the well-situated boulders and rocks of the traditional zen display. The sun-bleached and crazed blacktop of the parking lot lends a very American aesthetic to the Japanese version of precisely raked pebbles. Exchange students from the sister city, when visiting Winesburg, long to see the serene installation and arrange themselves on the perimeter, contemplating the possible narrative of juxtaposition before them. Arrayed artfully in a wide circle beyond the garden and the contemplative visiting observers, citizens of Winesburg, as they consider the landscape of loss and ruin in the static display before them, do not realize they too have contributed to the garden another layer of seeing and being seen.

# CARL FRANKENSTEIN, CUSTODIAN

I am a big man, a big man with an unfortunate name. The embroidery on my uniform stretches way beyond the pocket, oversews the placket. An ugly man who lives alone. A man who will not unlist his home phone number. A man who answers every phone call each night. "Frankenstein," I answer. I hear the murmuring laughs. At halftime of the basketball games, I lumber onto the hardwood with my wide furry mop, up and down the court. The students mob the stands, heave trash into my path. I circle, shaking my fists at the throng in the shadows of the bleachers, the monster I am. Their monster.

# CAROL CLAY

I look out for strays, and when I find them I take them
in. Our town of Winesburg has rows of telephone poles,
rows of electricity poles. The wires go every which way.
All wood, these poles, and I find my darlings clinging
there, their little claws dug deep in the pine, girdled
around at the same height like scallops of bark on a tree.
There is nothing sadder than the messages. Have you seen
the ones that say: Have you seen our Socks? Our Tom?
Our Kitty?? That ask: Have you seen Mr. Mittens?? Or
the ones that simply spell out LOST! or Reward!? Then
they go on to say (I need my glasses for this) what col-
or and how old and what special markings and last seen
and call us any time and we are sad and we miss miss
miss miss. I can't have enough of the missing. I pry them
free. I have a little flathead screwdriver to work under
the staple. I don't tear the paper. I'm allergic to the real
thing, to the real cat. But I fill my little house with these
cats with their ghost gray coats coating the pictures of
the flyers. I have x-acto-ed them from the sad news of
their departure. Look at that one yawning. That one's
eyes are flashed with light. That one covered with yarn.
Asleep in the sun. Batting a potted plant. Whaling on
a keyboard. All wet from a bath. I have albums of the
missing. In stacks and stacks though my bungalow, the
books themselves like cats warming themselves near the
registers, curled up on the coach, scratching at the door. I
have papered the walls with the paper—a choir, shingles
singing, mewing, purring. I open the door and the wall
ruffles, rustles, twitches, arches its back in the draft. Its
fur stands up. The fur flies. In some places, the paper is
several layers deep, and I can flip through and make the
kitties move, the still pictures fitting together into a movie
in my brain. They lick themselves and stretch. They chase

111

a bug. They roll and scratch. I go to the library to make more copies of my copies. I look sad. I've lost my cat. I am an old woman who has lost her cat. See, I show them. Have you seen Puddin'? They help me make copies of my copies. I put the pile in my red wagon. It is like walking a big red cat on a leash. Along the way, I look at all the poles, looking for new posters that ask me to look for missing cats. A tabby. A calico. Black cat. White cat. Long hair. Short. A Siamese. A Maine Coon cat. I have my little screwdriver to pry out the staple, to jimmy out the thumbtacks. I can't get enough. I paper over the windows of my bungalow with pictures of cats looking out the window. What are they looking at? Those cats are the inside cats. And I have taped more cats, outside cats, on the windows outside looking in at the inside cats. Cats are so curious. There are scare cats in my garden to scare the real cats away. Some pictures I have have more than one cat in them. Only one cat is missing but there are other cats pictured who aren't missing. I have found them all. The mommy cat who's nursing a brood of baby cats that now are all my cats. There are cats playing together. There are cats looking at goldfish in the goldfish bowl. Cats pawing at the refrigerator, at a bird flying by, at a child staring in. Many cats are sleeping. The big furry heads drooping. Ears are twitching in dreams. Tails flicking at the tip. Look, there the claws are extended. The cat is kneading. The outside light shines through the paper on the windows and pictures of cats curled up in a beam of sunlight curl up in the beam of sunlight cast through the window shadowed with pictures of cats chasing shadows. I have found all of these lost cats. The ones weathering on the light poles, on the telephone poles. I take pictures of the pictures and put the pictures in my albums, tape the pictures on the wall. When I am at the library, I copy the copy of a copy's copy. Each time the image of the cat licking its paw fades. It fades and fades. The light in the machine licks the paper on the glass bed. The copy's copy grays, breaks up into finer and finer pieces, shades and shades and shades and shades of gray. At night, I sleep in a bed made up with a bedding of lost cats, paper I have pieced together, page by page, into a quilted comforter of sleeping napping cats, a thrumming blanket. In the dark, I feel them nestle in next to me, hear them crinkle and crimp as I move as they move to nuzzle my ear, bat my hair. They fill in the hollows all around me. They flatten and slide beneath me. They surround me like a skin. They are my fur. They ride on my chest, lighter than light. They rise and fall as I breathe, finding in all the layers and layers of loss a way to be found.

# THE ANNUAL METAL DETECTOR MIGRATION

We are smack dab in the middle of the flyway, the great north/south corridor that runs between the beaches of the Gulf of Mexico on up into Michigan's iron rich mitten and the shingle shores of the UP. They arrive each spring in ones or twos, scouts we call them, a vanguard to the main flock that follows. Soon thereafter, the whole town of Winesburg is beset by murmurations of metal detectors in long lines, scalloped, wave on wave, their wands arching back and forth before them, their heads muffed with their earphones, lost within the sonic soundscape. They find a lot of nails and roof tacks, gum wrapper foil, and change, lots of change, especially in the streets near the parking meters where people, getting out of cars, going for coins in their pockets spill an extra dime or two in haste. For them, it's not worth it now to stoop and retrieve the leavings. Let it go to the migratory scavengers who will be here soon enough and who still relish the odd coin, a chance at finding a Mercury or buffalo among the dross in the margin, the gutter, the sidewalk crack. We watch them from our front porches as they sweep the streets and sidewalks silently. Many carry little shovels, beat-up trowels, cinch bags for bootie at the waist. They stare intently into the ground they tread as if they can see through the layers of accident and loss beneath their feet. And, of course, they can. They pantomime an archeology each visit, intent, listening for that ping of a thimble, a safety pin, a spring of coiled spring.

# HUNTER AND ART HUNT, STUDENT FUNDRAISERS

The thing is we have been selling these chocolate bars door-to-door in Winesburg for as long as we can remember. We used to like chocolate, but we don't anymore, having had to eat our consignment too many times. "Bring back empty boxes," is what we hear from Mrs. Wiggs our faculty advisor. She advised us to bring back empty boxes, and we took that to mean that if you couldn't sell all your consignment you had to buy the surplus yourself and eat it. It is hard to sell the chocolate after awhile. The town's not that big, and all the children in it are selling the same thing to the same people who are all the parents. We got a lot of different kinds of no-ing. You can see the bars of chocolate that got there before us in a pile on the floor of the front hall. The adults at the door looking down at us are always sad and a little angry. We think we are raising money for a field trip to someplace. We don't remember. Maybe South Bend. Maybe a toboggan ride at Pokagon. Maybe Muncie. We don't remember. We end up eating the candy ourselves. It's like eating the quilted skin of hand grenades. Long ago we gave up the dream of being the number one and two top sellers and winning a premium or two. Once, I wanted that Huffy bike, and Hunter, he'd go on and on, as we opened bar after bar, about those stilts that fit on the bottom of your shoes and lifted you up, a little bit, off the ground.

# SOMEONE IS PAINTING THE ELM TREES OF WINESBURG

There aren't that many left as you know. It is a blight. I like that word "blight." But that's neither here nor there. There are not that many elms left. Two or three here. A little grove there. But most are lone trees, remaining healthy, I imagine, by being quarantined from one another that way. When the blight first arrived and we knew nothing was to be done, we would sit with the dying trees, their serrated leaves turning yellow and falling when it wasn't even fall. It took a long time. We took turns with the one chainsaw we had, cutting down the dead dead trees and sectioning up the branches and trunks. We didn't know what to do with the cords. Didn't want to set the kindling on fire. The smoke perhaps would carry the contagion to the few remaining dying trees. When we weren't looking someone began painting the trees of Winesburg, a whitewash, waist high as if it was a demarcation of some flood, a high water mark. Perhaps it was a kind of magical thinking, turning the dying trees to ghosts before they give up the ghost. From a distance the girdle of paint creates an illusion. The dying trees seem to have severed themselves from their roots and are floating, levitating there a few feet above the infected ground. Or perhaps it is as if the trees are turning to stone, the trees becoming marble monuments of trees in increments. I think the whole trees should be blanched, but it seems all that the someone who is painting the trees can muster is this pale stain drained.

# HANK LINKLATER, TOWN TAPER

It's mostly a ceremonial position. I appear in all the pa-
rades, my pistol-gripped tape dispenser holstered smartly
on my hip. I keep a scanner tuned to the emergency channel. Sinkholes open up regularly and randomly, the bleat-
ing alarm horns of the autos swallowed whole calling and
responding all over town. I hustle from hole to hole, setting
up and cordoning off the collapses. The yellow tape gives
off its own light, it seems, but really it's all-reflective. Under
the dissipating beat of the horns you can hear the percussion of running water, the drip and gurgle. To me the tape
is a kind of civic adhesive. I am knitting up the community
with these second thoughts, this looking both ways. The
enclosures are our commons. Months later, I will return
to scenes of crimes I've taped to see the tape in tatters,
decaying, losing that yellow urgency, fading and foxing
in the sun. I'll tape that ruin with another perimeter of
warning, another circle outside the circle, another polygon
that frames the threadbare polygon from before. There is
a saying about painting the town red. But I tape the town
yellow, safety yellow. It's festive, if you think about it.

# VAN ZIMMER'S TREE ZOO

I'd like to say that the tree I have in the zoo is an endangered tree. It is one of the last elms or an American chestnut. An ash. Or the tree is an example of the state's official tree—the tulip poplar. Or say the tallest or oldest sycamore, or a sycamore transplanted here from the banks of the Wabash. But the tree is just a run-of-the-mill tree. A maple, I think. And not even a sugar bush maple. It is just a trash tree. What makes it special is this— for miles, it's the only tree left on this vast empty plain. You know grass is very smart. It has tricked us with its grain, its corn, into making war on the forests, clearing the fields of shade, uprooting roots. It wasn't like I even planted this specimen. It sprouted there in the grain bin, mulched by the ears and cobs. I like to watch those science shows on the TV, the ones that use time lapse film to record the way plants unfold, grow and bloom in the blink of an eye. I have been on this land for years and years, working the rotation. Beans to corn. Corn to beans. Beans to corn. Over and over. It's the least I can do to capture this one wild tree. Bottle it up. Impose upon it a kind or time quarantine, an embargo of place. In the fall, after the fields have been gleaned, I like to watch the tree's dyed leaves fall inside the cage. It's like television. Those leaves then get caught in there, and the wind agitates them, swirls them around and around inside the bin, scouring the whole thing with smears of color.

# THE CITY MANAGER: THE WEEPING WILLOW WINDBREAK OF WINESBURG

FDR himself came to Winesburg and planted the first few saplings. Well, he didn't actually plant them himself but sat up in the Sunshine Special and directed things. He wanted to build a grand shelterbelt from Canada to Mexico. We wanted to do our bit. The President motored away in that big old Lincoln, and he left a contingent of the CCC behind to finish the landscaping. That was years ago, and the shelterbelt was never really realized in the aggregate. But here in Indiana there is this little baffle of depression-era willows. Roosevelt was haunted by the roiling clouds of dust, dreamed of something to knock the dirt out of the thin air. Well, the wind is with us here. We always say there is nothing to slow it down, the wind, as it slides off the mountains out west. There was an oracle in ancient Greece where the priests got their instructions in the rustle of the breeze in the leaves. Oak leaves, I believe. The lachrymose leaves of the willow are all muffled, mumbling mostly. They are pretty to look at, I suppose, this memorial copse, this limping crippled orchard smudging the horizon.

# GLEN RETINGER'S SURPLUS BARRAGE BALLOON

I kept it in the barn. But I hauled it out for all the holidays, on full moon nights, playing out its cables slowly
letting the balloon come about, join the clouds another kind of cloud. After the war there were thousands of
them, surplus, some never even used. Mine came packed
in cosmoline. Recently it has become more difficult pro-
curing the helium now that Congress privatized the chemical and closed the federal helium depot in Texas. I played
the market, hedged, speculated on helium futures. That's
where it all went sideways. I visit the envelope (that's
what we call it, the envelope) in the barn as it slowly
deflates. I can't keep it patched. The seams are the worst.
It is good to know that it is an inert gas. No need to fear
combustion. The gas just goes, giving up the ghost. I have
to say there is a kind of high derived from the high squeak
that leaks out of you when under the influence. Civil asset
forfeiture it's called when the cops arrest your property
along with yourself. There will be a case soon, The United States of America vs. Glen Retinger's Barrage Balloon.
Once it seemed so innocent, my balloon, a wonderment.
Now it's one deflation after another. A shit storm. A train
wreck or a balloon wreck that just keeps happening. All
hell breaking loose.

# THE NATIONAL MOURNERS UNION, LOCAL 440

Who will mourn us, unionized mourners, when the Funeral Directors, Cemetery Sextons, Dioceses and Congregations break us? We are locked out already, outside looking in at the scab mourners graveside. We might as well be ghosts the way the processions and corteges blow through our picket lines. There is a method to mourning, the sadness sculpted by our own experience of grief, of course, but also the daily craft of keening we hone with the strop of constant sorrow. Our weeping might be practiced but it is sincere, and our demands are not extreme. A living wage is all we ask to sustain our professional attention to all this dying. We spend the time down at the union hall passing the time, remembering the good and the bad—our apprenticing, our journeyman days, our active memberships, our overtimes of tears, trying to convince ourselves that this is a mere rehearsal; a run through of a wake. Not the wake itself.

# DAN HOWELL, BUILDING THE GREAT WALL OF WINESBURG

Of course, I want this wall to be seen from outer space like that other great wall in China. I am not sure, though, if I am constructing this wall with a purpose of keeping people from coming in or keeping people from going out. I am positive that I want the wall to run the whole circuit of the city. Later, I will think about dry moats, glacis, ramparts, ravelins, tenailles, hornworks or crown works, and bastions, lots of bastions. I will build a model in the shed sculpted out of sugar cubes and rejected block erasers from the eraser factory. So out there in space, you'll look down from the stars to see my star fort. Course after course. Orchards of plumb lines. And yet I am still not sure where the danger is coming from, inside or out. Perhaps this star will collapse in upon itself, turn itself inside out. A big black hole, so big it can be seen, or not seen, from outer space.

# THE BIOMET SECONDS OUTLET

Further west, up US 30, The Lincoln Highway, in Warsaw is the headquarters and main manufactory of the Biomet Company, the premier producer of artificial hips and knees, electronic stimulators, and other prosthetic and therapeutic hardware. In Winesburg, Biomet operates a seconds and slightly used retail outlet along with a refurbishing shop. We don't have much walk-in traffic. That's a joke we like to repeat. We don't get much walk-in traffic. The days are long in the store, and we have to keep ourselves entertained because, as you know, we don't get much walk-in traffic. During those long empty shifts I like to test the joints, articulate them, clicking the hinge of an alloy knee, ratcheting through the whole range of motion. I toggle the hip's ball and socket like a stick shift. The time passes. Click. Click. It is self-hypnosis. A kind of mindfulness, I imagine. I consider the tarnish, the patina, the stain on the stainless steel, how it wasn't there and then, in a moment, rust. In the quiet through the hum of the lights I think I hear the world grinding away outside, bone on bone. The dust shifts through the reversed engineered sunlight breaking into splinters of color. The day takes itself apart out there. There it goes, piece by piece.

# FORREST NORTON, CAMERA OPERATOR, GOOGLE STREET VIEW

It is impossible to get lost in northeastern Indiana. I've tried. But everywhere is the grid. The grid is everywhere. I travel north to south, south to north on the section roads. Up and down. Over and back. It is a landscape of prepositions. I have to have the GPS link on at all times, synching with the photos I am taking, but you don't really need a satellite to let you know where where is here. The land itself looks like a map of itself, a 1:1 correspondence. No projection at all. No skew along one axis or other. Thomas Jefferson, who came up with the idea of the township, thought the grid to be the most democratic of patterns. I don't know. I've heard that out there somewhere colleagues of mine are documenting the intersection of every intersection of major latitudes and longitudes the world over, and all the photographs are out there too on the World Wide Web. Most of them are in the middle of some ocean. At night, after a day of panoramic boredom, I click through that file. Sea. Sea. Sea. Sea. It's a kind of geographic pornography, I guess. I get lost in all that sameness. A chart for the sensory deprived, a glimpse of the forbidden.

# THE MOSQUITO TRUCK OF WINESBURG

There is something wrong with the passenger side tire. The truck is a late model and comes equipped with an air pressure sensor. It seems it always happens about the same time each dusk as I am drifting through the neighborhoods. The light will flicker on, a flat half moon floating in the speedometer dial. It pisses me off. I have to recalculate my route through the dying ash trees. Did I tell you the ash trees are dying? The ash trees are dying. It's a borer, an insect it seems unaffected by the fog I am generating. I make my way to a gas station I know has an air pump. I am there on my hands and knees, the flashlight in my teeth, working the nozzle onto the stem of the deflating tire, the apparatus in the bed still steaming, sending up a cloud like a thought balloon, the thrum of its generator talking back to the generator on the air pump. Tomorrow, I tell myself, I will get this rig up on a rack and eyeball the treads looking for the source of this slow leak—a roofers nail, I bet, a loose bolt, a wood screw buried in the rubber. Who knows what's all scattered on the ground, what's fallen out of nowhere, waiting there to find the tangent of my nightly rounds.

# PICKY DASHNER, SLOW POUR OIL CHANGE

It is, finally, a better change of oil the slower the oil is changed. It should take four hours or more, mostly more. That time passes for me in the pit below your car or truck. I'm in the semi-dark below your semi, the slow drip drip drip of your draining spent lubricant. There, there is plenty of time to consider time. How the old oil seeping from the pan is itself very old. Coniferous fossil fluid squeezed out of the past, vintage, pine, a distillation of the slipperiness of pressed time's passing. I like the oily dark, here down under, an inkling. It is always cooler in the pit and here I sit and steep. In the cave dark the silence between the plinking drips extends to the point there is an infinity of infinities between this second and then the second second, the sleep of sensory deprivation. And then I plug the pan, and somewhere plumb above, someone funnels in the new oil, and I, still in the dark, see, cave paintings of a sort, the charcoal etchings of the baffles and cams, the infinitesimal crawl of the coating the nooks and crannies of the gaskets and shafts, the sleeves of cylinders washed with a coating the thickness of one graphic graphite molecule deep. It is deep down in this deep. I heard once, a long time ago, that the monks down at St. Meinrad sleep in their coffins. I am awake in my grave.

# CARRIE CRABTREE, PAWPAW GROWER

I have to hand pollinate since the flower isn't much to smell. Something so sweet, it's vaguely rotten. But there's not enough putrefaction to attract the blowflies, carrion beetles. The swallowtail caterpillar, the pawpaw leaves is all it eats but never in enough numbers to make a dent in what's needed. I do like to see the dazzled clouds of butterflies sift through the big flat leaves of the pawpaw at dawn. Did I mention you need at least one other variety (I like Wabash) to set fruit? Well, you do. I've tried hanging a chicken neck next to the blossom, but it was a no go. Out come my tweezers. The pawpaw is a pudding fruit. Quite tasty. It is a big seller in Winesburg, eaten right there by the truck. People bring their own spoons. The fruit doesn't store. It ferments right away. Plucking it is like pulling a pin on a hand grenade. Ticking time bomb is what it is. Pawpaw. Pawpaw. Boom. But there is something about that taste on your tongue right there on the edge of going bad that makes it so good.

# THE FULLER BRUSH MAN

I might be the last one left, selling brushes door to door. And I have been at it long enough that I think I know every door in town. I know every chip and tint of tarnish of the doorknockers, the way the doorbell buttons dim when depressed, the tears in the seams of each screen door. I know they are in there. I can hear them breathing. But they know I am out on the stoop, the porch, the steps with my bag. Everyone needs a brush. You can't have enough brushes. Everywhere you look there is the daily grime and grit, dust and dirt, rust and rot. Here are some of the brushes I sell: toothbrushes, floor brush, yard brush, yard broom, hand brush scrubber, shoe-polish buffer, curling brush, nail brush, milk-churn brush, vacuum-cleaner brush, archaeology brush, lavatory brush, vegetable brush, clothes brush, gun-barrel brush, wire brush, typewriter eraser brush, dandy brush, dishwashing brush, bench-grinder brush, flue brush, chimney brush, bottle brushes, brooms of all kinds which are just long-handled brushes, paintbrushes, wall-paper brush, shoe-polish brush, makeup brushes, mascara brush, nail-polish brush, finger-print brush, pastry brush, ink brush, shaving brush, gilding brush. You name it; I got it. Or I can get it for you. I walk the streets of Winesburg. Once, there were a lot of us. I palled around with the Electro Lux guy for years, swapping dirt, not gossip but real bags of dirt, for demonstrations. Now, it's just me and the knife grinder, the sharpener, who wheels his grinding stone around. He never knocks on doors but shouts from the streets. I try to shoo him away. He cramps my style. "Shoo," I say, "shoo, shoo."

# FLEGLER'S INTERIOR DESIGN

We specialize in wall coverings of all kinds of course. You don't have to twist my arm too much and I will be there with a stencil and roller. I've even been known to do a block printing or two with stamps I've cut myself in the rejected cake erasers from the Pink Pearl plant. But we are featuring all this month the newest wallpaper in the Seismic line, wallpaper designed to stabilize masonry walls preventing them from failing during earthquakes! The product has been around since 2012. Artists at the Institute of Solid Construction and Construction Material Technology of the Karlsruhe Institute of Technology were spitballing, threw the ideal against the wall, so to speak, to see if it would stick. The paper uses glass fiber reinforcement in several directions and a special adhesive. The pattern is my own design—a sonogram of Yodeling Slim Clark yodeling "Big Rock Candy Mountain." There's a lot of worries in Winesburg, and earthquakes are one of them. Why would they not be? Now I am no psychologist, but the ambient anxiety all around is wearing. I like to think by treating the interiors of the sad and shaky spaces we inhabit we all will also live better within our own scarred and tattooed skins. But that could just be me.

# RUEL COAL & ICE

There's not much call for coal no more. Or ice now that I think about it. Once the two fit together like, well, coal and ice. The business was just about hauling solid blocks of stuff always on the edge of turning into something else. There's still the pond outside of town with the siding where the Pennsy set out a cut of cars. We iced the reefers there and then. And in the season we transshipped the coal the hoppers dumped in the bins. We still sell a scuttle or two. Someone has a potbelly in the tool shed. There's the one oven at the bakery. You know the alleys of Winesburg were paved in cinders, clinkers from the coal. I remember the smoke leaked up into the sky raking the clouds all over town. We hauled the ashes as well. Now our revenue is realized through renting the roof out to antenna arrays, microwaves to mine the sized electromagnetic soup. It's just another state of matter. Invisible? Sure. Welcome to my goddamn sublime apocalypse.

# THE CITY MANAGER: SUNSET CONTRAIL VIEWING

It has something to do with the topography, the atmospherics hereabouts. The lake effect. The flatness. The temperamental barometric pressures that percolate from the numerous Belted Galloway herds of the neighborhood. The distorted magnetic fields. The transpiration of the corn crop. The thermal inversions generated by the vast murmurations of starlings. Somehow the contrails emitted by the day's jet traffic overhead all over America end up aloft above Winesburg. It's a kind of cloud sump, a vapor drain. It is what we do hereabouts most nights, view the train wrecks of the contrails, the collisions and the congestion. It brings us a kind of comfort. Comfort. Suspended fossils of time. Ruins of the long gone.

# THE BAT BOXES OF WINESBURG, INDIANA

I like bats. You can say I am the number one fan of the Indiana Bat. The Indiana Bat—a little guy, a quarter of an ounce, the weight of four dimes. But it has a fatal flaw. Not its size. Its size is fine. No. Its fatal flaw is how it hibernates each winter in these droves of 50,000 or more in the caves hollowed out around Winesburg, here in the northernmost reaches of the limestone karst of Indiana. But that is still okay. Their small size, their vast numbers. No, it's the white nose syndrome that's at them. And none of us knows what is up with that. So I build bat houses to help out. I encourage my neighbors to do the same. During summer they roost under the peeling bark of dead and dying trees. And the plywood boxes mimic that natural delamination. The bats hang out in habitats of small river and stream corridors of mature riparian woods. So I build the boxes within a few miles of the branches of the western fork of the Fork River as they disappear in sinkholes underground. In the summer, the lighting bugs spark off of the branches of the understory, the dogwood and redbud. The swallows and the swifts jink and swoop in the dusk. And the Indiana Bats sift out of the baffles of the bat houses like the litter of leaves, like saw dust from some unseen sanding.

# CARSON CARLSON, LINOLEUM INSTALLER

I don't install linoleum. I install polyvinyl chloride in sheets or tiles. It's a common mistake. Completely different material but it doesn't matter. "Linoleum" comes from the Latin for flax, *linum*, and the Latin for oil, *oleum*. It just sounds better beneath your feet than, say, polyvinyl chloride. Linoleum. The mumbling of a Latin mass. I used to correct people when they made the mistake. At times coming close to blows. It's a common mistake. I was a stickler once for the technically correct term. I have my pride. A professional, a propriety thing. But over time I let it go. I install a plastic after all. I am, let's say, pliable. Linoleum. Certain words wear a pattern. Spring to mind. Linoleum. Become, um, harmonic. A kind of hum.

# THE COUNTY EXTENSION AGENT

It is just a grass, corn, a grass gone wild. And, it seems, every corner of this corner of Indiana (a corner flat as a flat iron flattened by the ironing glaciers making for the ideal landscape for the grass) is plaited by the plant. It looks so innocent. But we are warned, when we are knee high to the 4th of July, not to venture into the amazing maze of the mature field of maize. It doesn't matter though. Every summer, a toddler will toddle into some seam of a corn row, a corn row with the ripe ten-foot flying buttress-y stalks stitching together an opaque canopy overhead. It's a cinch the kid is lost. And we have to go in after, walking the mile long row, losing track of the lookers in the rows on either side. It's all scale, and you yourself shrink as you yourself search, shrink to the point where you yourself are lost at seeing, disoriented and adrift, listing, sinking. You yourself begin to see things.

# ZANDOR SANDS, HOMEOWNER

Every time after I take a shower, I squeegee down the fiberglass walls of the stall. You don't want the beads of water to be left behind to evaporate. It leaves a film, a kind of ghost, of dissolved soap that can build up over time into a real scum. The squeegeeing takes care of that. It leaves behind a pristine dry surface as if you never took a shower in the first place. I have a whole routine worked out. I like to make sure the swipe of one pass laps over the edge of the previous sweep. In this way I get every last bead of water. Oh, and it is different on the glass of the shower doors. You squeegee off the steam and yet the glass is still diffused but not as diffused as it was before you squeegeed off the glass. My father taught me this. To squeegee. He wanted me to squeegee the tiles of the bath surround at home, and I did. He might have even given me the squeegee I use now to squeegee my own shower stall walls. A housewarming gift of sorts. I think he did, yes. I use the squeegee on everything now. Windows, of course. The house's siding after it rains as mildew can build up outside as well as inside. You know, it is something. Every time I squeegee, and that's almost every day, I think of my old man. It's one of the many things he worried about when he was alive, all those tears accumulating ahead of that elaborate elastic squeak.

# JANE QUIGLEY, DOCENT, THE QUONSET HUT MUSEUM

There I am, years ago, soon after The War, when we—my husband John and I—finished the construction of the second of two Quonset Huts that made up the original Quonset Hut Museum in Winesburg, Indiana. This was the unit we lived in. You'll notice that it was a duplex. My sister, Jean, and her husband, James Quigley, lived in the other half of the hut. John and James, both Marines, served in The War, but, after The Sullivans, couldn't serve together. James found himself stationed on Adak Island in the Aleutian Chain and John was bivouacked a half a world away on Tristan da Cunha. During The War, Jean and I worked at the Eraser Factory in Winesburg, converted for the duration from producing block and pencil tip erasers to the production of prophylactic condoms.

Lodged at the ends of the earth and with their girls back home in Indiana—the center vertex, so to speak, of the Great Circle the points of their locations described—they dreamed beneath the arching wall-into-ceiling-into-wall vault of the Quonset Huts that sheltered them for four years. Unbeknownst to each other, both brothers separately concluded the same thing—that if he should survive, he would return to the center of the world—Winesburg, Indiana—and valorize the habitat that housed him. Today, years after The War, the brothers, both in their nineties, still venture ever outward in ever widening circles in search of more surviving examples of the type that remain in, what they call, The Wild. They ship the parts back home—the corrugated steel pieces scalloped on the museum's grounds, expressing that constant 2.4-meter radius that mimics the distant curvature of the earth the rest of us see as a mere horizontal horizon.

# STU MADDEN'S GAZING BALL BARN

It's not as if I grow them on purpose. But they do seem to appear suddenly in the fields. Like a weed. I think of them as volunteers. It used to be, before the Round Up, that we would walk the beans around here. The whole neighborhood would, well, volunteer to hoe out the volunteers in the new stand of crop. If this were a bean field then the weed, the volunteer, would be a rogue corn plant left over from the season's rotation before. It was now a weed in the bean field, and you'd go in there and root out these little geysers of green amongst the sprouting legumes. But then we just switched over to the chemical and the genetic genies in the discombobulated seeds. Well sir, you didn't need any neighbors no more to walk no beans. I broadcast the herbicide with a sprayer on an old red Harvester H I have. I rumble through the field floating on the fog of its dispersing. After I am done with the application, I contemplate the treated field from what was once the fence line. The fences are long gone too. In the days we walked a field, the cleaned-up row of cultivated beans made a pleasing stand. Now I am a little bit saddened by the fact that though the weeds will die in a day or two, for now, the vegetation is still all vegetably, not cleaned up at all. I stall on the lip of a ditch and contemplate the beans. I see in the settling clouds of poison, I think, the crowds of ghosts of all my long gone neighbors. I can stare into that verdant but vacant field for hours. And then, in a day or two, about the time it takes for the volunteers to be all desiccated, dissolving into the ground, I will see the sprout or three or more of what grows into these ornamental gazing ball like shrubs, with this big fruit of neon green or red or blue or sliver, that seem too to be impervious to the ready remedies. The Purdue extension agent suspects it's the *boketto*. He tells me it is an Asian pest of some sort, invasive, and without its natural predators, resistant, so far, to any treatment. They ripen right there in the field, and I harvest them by hand, hoe them out alone now. The stalks will destroy the header on the combine. I dry them down in the sunlight. Even though I have many things to do this time of the year, (I have many things to do almost any time of the year) I can't keep my eyes off them.

# THINGS

Things was, at one time, quite the thing in Winesburg. It was the notions store when there was still interest in domestic sewing, home haberdashery. Its bins, drawers, shelves, cabinets, displayed tables contained all kinds of things—bias tape, grommets, collar stays, rickrack, twill tape, piping, selvedge, tracing wheels, thimbles, pinking shears, pattern notchers, hook-and-eyes, awls, tape measures, zippers, elastic, interfacing, eyelets, trim, fringe, ribbon, thread, yarn, snaps, toggles, buckles, needles, needle threaders, darning eggs, pins, buttons (all kinds of buttons)—covered buttons, ceramic, frogs, hair, intaglio, enameled, worked, plastic, shell, vegetable ivory, metal, filigree, electroplated, wood, mica—fabrics, clews, patterns. Things and things. You can still see ghosts of mannequins and dress forms through the soaped windows. There are just so many things to keep track of, of which to keep track. I can't bring myself to liquidate the inventory even though no one for some time has taken any notion of notions. In the back office I make lists. I make lists of lists. I fear I am losing the ability to name the names of things. That the particular permutation of letters that make up names to name names is evaporating. One day, I fear, I will only have, lodged in the cabinets of my brain, a list of things. This thing. This thing. This thing. And this. This thing thing here. This thing thing there. All the things of Things just things.

# THE CITY MANAGER: THE GIRLHOOD HOME OF ZERNA SHARP

The house, located at 44 Zerna Street (Maple Street having been renamed in her honor) was the girlhood home of Zerna Sharp, author of the Dick and Jane Readers. However, the house located at 44 Zerna Street is not the actual girlhood home of Zerna Sharp, author of the Dick and Jane Readers. The house located at 44 Zerna Street is actually a replica of the house that was located at 44 Maple Street (later renamed Zerna Street in honor of Zerna Sharp, author of the Dick and Jane Readers) when Zerna Sharp, author of the Dick and Jane Readers lived there as a child. The actual house at 44 Zerna Street that Zerna Sharp, author of the Dick and Jane readers, lived in as a girl and that is now replaced by a replica is currently located at Henry Ford's Greenfield Village, located in Dearborn, Michigan, outside of Detroit, Michigan. Henry Ford's Greenfield Village, located in Dearborn, Michigan, outside of Detroit, Michigan, collects and preserves many houses that once were houses of important American inventors and artists as well as many other historic structures and artifacts such as windmills, train depots, one room school houses (where Zerna Sharp, the author of the Dick and Jane Readers, first distributed the Dick and Jane Readers), and the hat Lincoln was wearing the night he was assassinated. In 1932, Henry Ford, moved the actual girlhood home of Zerna Sharp, author of the Dick and Jane Readers, to Greenfield Village in Dearborn, Michigan, outside of Detroit, Michigan. It was discovered, years later, that Henry Ford when he moved the girlhood home of Zerna Sharp, author of the Dick and Jane Readers, to Greenfield Village in Dearborn, Michigan, outside of Detroit, Michigan, did not do so knowing it was the girlhood home of Zerna Sharp, author of the

Dick and Jane Readers, but instead believed the house, at what was then 44 Maple Street, was a fine example of the Carpenter Gothic Style of vernacular American domestic architecture, sending it (in one piece) to Greenfield Village in Dearborn, Michigan, outside of Detroit, Michigan. Tours of the replica of the girlhood home of Zerna Sharp, author of the Dick and Jane readers, located at 44 Zerna Street, are by appointment only.

# NIKKI TEMONE, PBX OPERATOR, THE GERBER HAUS MOTEL

I also am the night auditor, and the machine I use to audit is as antiquated as the switchboard behind the front desk. The NCR 442 is nothing but a glorified cash register. Every night—it doesn't matter—the house is always out of balance. At four in the morning, I will still be looking through the long long long long tapes for the stupid mistake a clerk made during the day. More often than not, an absent-minded inversion of the tail numbers of the balance pick up. I am always "off" by a number divisible by nine. You can always tell. It's magic that way. I work through the night. I log all the wake-up calls. I have a clock that lets me set alarms every 15 minutes. The buzzing goes off, well, like clockwork, and I run to the PBX. I socket home the wire and toggle the switch to ring the room. "Good morning," I say in my quiet voice, "it's four a.m. and this is your wake-up call." If no one answers, I have to go to the room and make sure everyone's awake. The policy of the property. Most times, people have already left. Or the shower's running when I peek in to ask "Are you up?" But here's the thing. Suicides always leave wake-up calls. They want to be found. They don't want to be found found. Not found in time. But found soon after time. I think about this while I am running the room and tax with the NCR 442 in trial mode. I am the night auditor, and I listen to all that nothing through the night.

# MARVIN PUFF MOTORS

I gave up on the "motors" long ago. I was a Studebaker dealer once. I stuck around for parts and service. Then my inventory dwindled to small engines, two-stroker Briggs and Stratton that kind of thing. Now I lot used shopping carts mostly, specializing in the classic lines. No new-fangled plastic for me. I hold an auction on the Labor Day weekend like Kruse does up in Auburn for those Cords and Duesenbergs. Folks come from all over to bid on the finely restored powder-coated aluminum mesh Goldman Piggly Wiggly or a string of Oral Watsons nesting one into the other. I like the nesting. The way they fit just so. The rest of the year I like to trick out a folding baby shelf or two, lining the seat with fake fur, a sound system. I might get back into the motor business now that the buggies are becoming self-propelled. Little traction motors that purr. The folks at Rogers market let me use their aisles as a test track at night after hours. You'll find me there in the stale fluorescent lamp light. One of the wheels on the test bed always flat. The other one with a stutter in the bearings. The raspberry, I call it, that rattle in the shadows of the end caps, leaving that telltale skid in the vinyl tiling as I corner into the cold steaming meat bins.

145

# THE CITY MANAGER: THE INGMAR BERGMAN DRIVE-IN THEATRE

One will find on the outskirts of Winesburg the Ingmar Bergman Drive-In Theatre. It is a repertoire theater exclusively showing the films of the great Swedish writer/director, Ingmar Bergman. *Through a Glass Darkly*, *The Silence*, *Winter's Light*, *Wild Strawberries*, *Cries and Whispers*, *The Seventh Seal*, *The Magic Flute* and *Fanny and Alexander* as well as every episode of "Scenes from a Marriage" television series are shown, rotating through the summer nights, in the original Swedish. It is a rite of passage for the students from Durkheim High to sneak into the venue by hiding in the trunks of cars to view the films free of charge. The Ingmar Bergman Drive-In Theatre is well attended not only for its provocative and moving series of movies but because the drive-in occupies a special precinct in time. By a special executive order of the governor of the State of Indiana, the Ingmar Bergman Drive-in Theatre is exempt from Daylight Saving Time. The clock that runs on the screen marking time to the beginning of the feature assuring you there is time to still make it to the concession stand, is a time unto itself. The couples in the cars, sprawled out on rough blankets spread on car hoods, the kids swinging on the swing sets, all sense the distortion in time and space as tinny Swedish dialogue leaks out over the field from the choir of car speakers.

# KENDRA KLEIN, BUDDHIST

Everyday I translate this poem:

古池や蛙飛こむ水のおと

old pond
frog jump into
water sound

But that's not right. So I do it again.

old pond
frog jump into
water sound

There is a little drumlin at the edge of Winesburg. I walk out there early in the morning. I take a gig with me just in case. The water is as smooth as a mirror. A mirror on a tabletop. I remember when I was young, and I was prescribed contact lenses. I held my lids apart while balancing the crisp lens on my one free finger. I looked at my eye looking at the lens on my free finger as it approached the lens of my eye. Closer and closer until. The sliver of plastic snapped across the gap, all attraction, fluid to fluid, quicksilver. And there was, in that moment, a tiny tsk as the lens found its socket, stuck. A sonic drip. I blinked hard, squeegeed the surplus solution off the mote, a torn tear tearing out of there. And ever since then, I always say, I have had something in my eye, a something where, within each blink, I hear the irritation, that precious little pearl of pain, that lisping blister.

# ALICE TANG, COMPETITIVE CLOTHESPIN PINNER

We say the wind in Indiana is so strong because there is nothing to slow it once it slides down the dry side of the Rockies. My backyard is rigged with dozens of ropes and strings and wires all waiting to be strung with clothes. I prefer to call them clothes pegs instead of pins, and I peg up the sopping sheets in record time. Northern Indiana is the Bonneville Salt Flats of clothespin pinning. My laundry blooms into sails luffing, lofting, spilling the wind in bushel baskets of breeze. I dream of clipper ships, of making way. Watch me go! I am on a reach, reaching the laundry over the sag. One peg crimps one seam of one garment to the hem of the next one and so on and so on. It's so endless. I twist in the wind. I disappear in the maze of scalded cotton, the baffle of crazy quilts. This evaporation. This congested absence. This expiration. This stiff wind.

# THE 141st ACOUSTIC BATTALION (EARLY'S EARS), INDIANA NATIONAL GUARD

*Fort Lew Wallace, Winesburg, Indiana, Armory*

We train every other weekend, listening to the static of silence. Have you ever really heard the quilted quiet of Indiana? The traffic on the toll road rolls in, a whispering hush, like wave on waves on some sand beach somewhere. We home in on the hisses of a kitten in Ohio. We're deafened by the brooding sawing of cicada emerging in mass from their papery blisters scaling the dying elm trees in Fort Wayne. It is the sonic signature of dying, the blight, we can hear the cells themselves dividing in the fungi (is it a fungi?) as it multiplies, a kind of sizzle. Listen, that bare nothing is the thunder generated by the stuttering lisp of this summer's heat lighting. Yes, that's it. That's it exactly.

# SIMON GLUCK: MIDGET RACER RACER

I like to go down to Fort Wayne and race my midget racer indoors at the Memorial Coliseum Indoor Midget Racer Races. I never win. But I love the vectors of the physical laws of the universe—how bodies in motion stay in motion—impressed upon me as I skid on the high banks and into the soggy hay bales at the lip. I did win once. It was the Winesburg, Indiana, Gran Prix. All the other Midget Racer Racers crashed or broke down or ran out of gas or simply lost interest and made a wrong turn and got lost in Winesburg's back alleys.

# THE FLYWAY OF BLUE TRUCKS

Ruth Cameron's father, Edgar, built this 200-foot-high tower on the outskirts of Winesburg, Indiana, in the early days of the Second World War to spot (what was widely believed at the time) the coming aerial bombardment by the Nazi Luftwaffe. Ruth scanned the sky well into 1948, suspicious that reports of Victory in Europe might not be accurate. Today, her Zeiss optics binoculars are turned earthward as she tracks the traffic on the old Lincoln Highway, recording the parade of blue trucks (North American Van Lines livery) as it enters into and leaves out of the headquarters city of Fort Wayne. She keeps track of all the households hubbing through that city, the lumbering blue trucks idling in the breakdown lanes as they wait for instructions to rendezvous with one another in the empty parking lots of ruined city and shuffle their cargoes from one van to another under the cover of darkness.

# THE CITY MANAGER: THE WINESBURG BLEACHATORIUM

Researchers from the astrophysics department of Indiana-Purdue University Fort Wayne suspect the tear in the fabric of space and time began with a denim thread found in the lint trap of dryer number 4 thirteen years ago. The laundry has been monitored ever since by teams of graduate assistants, cloaked in off-white white lab coats, sprawled on molded fiberglass side chairs, passing the time leafing through dog-eared and water-stained periodicals in the flickering narrow spectrum light whose bleak photons are always approaching the underwhelming event horizon forming over the boomerang patterned Formica-clad folding table in the corner . . .

# GREGG PITMAN

The third "g," the double on the end, is not a misspelling. That is how you spell my name. I am a bastard. My father was a visiting stenography instructor, my night school mother's teacher at Winesburg's Business Athenaeum. I was conceived in the simulated office suite on the second floor whose desks had all been graffitied with the swooping swooshes and schwa strokes of its students studying Shorthand. In short, Shorthand became my first language. With the sharpened red-painted nail of her index finger, my mother, never speaking, transcribed what she was thinking on my belly or on my back as I learned to toddle or on my butt as she changed me. In Shorthand, she annotated me with her abbreviated and compressed baby talk in the style of gestural dingbats, curlicues, and ellipses of this our secret shared language. My growth was stunted by this stunted dialect, abbreviated, and, at the same time, accelerated as Shorthand was built for speed. I never, really, learned to speak—my grammar truncated, my vocabulary condensed, the syntax reduced like a roux—but I did learn to listen. Listen: I turned out to have the gift of anticipation. I am a kind of hobbled psychic who only foresees a few seconds into the future, enough to change the story before it is told or, at least, to get the gist of the gist down on paper. It was only natural that I ended up doing what I am doing now. I'm the municipality's court reporter, a freelance clerk at all the depositions, a civil servant, an auxiliary in the interrogation rooms of the constabulary, recording the endless confessions of the long-winded citizenry whose secrets of incest, abuse, murder, rape, and torture pile-up in the coded squiggles and squirms of my spiral bound oblong pads. At night in my shotgun shack on the West End, I reread the traumatic digestions of trauma, note how all these horrific acts have been transformed, strike that, I meant to say tamed, by their abstraction into the innocent scratches of a child pretending to write. I cannot sleep. Or when I do, I dream of a writing orgiastic montage of writing run amuck. I wake to moonlight. There, crescent moon is a silent letter in the Shorthand of the universe. It stands for "and" or "but" or "or." Sleepless, I compose grosses of bad news letters for the front office of the Winesburg Knitting Mill, using the supplied templates of boilerplate text, leaving blank the spaces for the recipient and the sender to be supplied by the cursive endless longhand of the anonymous signatory.

# THE CITY MANAGER: THE HOTEL FORT WAYNE

The one high-rise in Winesburg, the old Hotel Fort Wayne, has long been abandoned. It sits derelict on the edge of downtown, casting shadows over the less storied buildings below. There is no money to tear it down. Its demolition has been an agenda item of the city council for years now. Perhaps it will be rehabbed, turned into a retirement condo for the aging population. Winesburg is aging. Perhaps an Art Center. Winesburg is the only municipality in the country that supports a company performing historic tableau. Maybe a museum, The Museum of Ruin, dedicated to decay. We will need a curator to arrange the exhibits of evaporation, erosion, desiccation. We will need a maintenance staff to maintain the steady decline. There will be a gift shop featuring objects whose purpose or meanings have been forgotten or lost. There will be a cloakroom where visitors' wraps and hats, umbrellas and overshoes once stored, will not be found again.

# THE WINDMILL GARDEN

Cyrus Backrum, walking on the Great Glacial Plain west of Winesburg, Indiana, watched as engineers from the Wrigley Chewing Gum Company attempted to make even more level the level fields stretching out all around them. The gum company hoped to make more efficient and productive land on which to grow crops of spearmint and peppermint. The engineers used laser levels to survey and mark the minute gradients, the eerie red beams of light criss crossing the vast empty openness. It was at this moment that Mr. Backrum received a revelation of sorts as the front-page broadsheet of yesterday's Denver Post newspaper blew into his face, slapping him with enough force to send him to the ground. The paper, he realized had traveled unmolested, propelled on its true vector by the prevailing wind from the Mile High City to this rendezvous with destiny. He resolved immediately to establish a Windmill Garden on the spot where the contraptions he planted would not lift water or generate electricity but do nothing more than mill the ceaseless wind, making visible the mint-scented invisible breath of the Lord God Almighty Himself.

# THE PAINT TESTING FIELDS

At noon in the summer, we like to go to the paint testing fields on the north side of Winesburg, Indiana, and picnic near the racks of paint strips and samples as they weather. We swear that some days we can see the paint fade before our eyes. The glossy ones especially grow dull as we watch, chewing our sandwiches like cud. We don't know why this is so. Winesburg is never really sunny as we are situated in the long shadow of Lake Michigan's climate, its Lake Effect infecting us all, we guess.

# SETH POLLIN'S WHITE ELEPHANT

Once, I traded in everything, in everything plus one. But now I just collect kitchen sinks. They are, for me, the Alpha and the Omega. I spend my days plumbing them all together. Gallons of water I divert from the west fork of the Fork River circulate through the growing hydraulic system. There are sinks sinking into sinks. Everything, yes, everything is swallowed. Everything drained. Everything twisted twisting. Everything, plus me, turned inside out. Or outside in.

# LANG SPANGLE, GHILLIE SUIT AFICIONADO

How do you like my ghillie suit? Do you think it disrupts my silhouette? Is it more difficult to distinguish the figure from the ground? Have I been able to capture the proper technique of countershading? Can you see me? Is it confused? The highlight? The shadow? How is the light falling on what would be, if you could see it, my shoulder? How long have I been standing here in the courthouse square? Did you notice me there? Were you confused, for a moment, thinking I was a statue of a person in a ghillie suit instead of a person in a ghillie suit standing still as a statue? Or did you think I was shrubbery? A bush? Silage? Compost? At night, under the cover of darkness, do I disappear in a different way? Is my mother continuing to look for me? Has my father given up the search? My family, do they wonder, I wonder, about me still? Do you see through me? Do I bend the light around me? Does that light scatter? Does it get absorbed? Do I blend in as I stand out?

# PLEIN AIR PAINTER

I am the local plein air painter, May Mavro, I perform drawing studies of the contents of Winesburg's eraser factory's aggregate depot. Ingredients used in making the erasers arrive daily from all over the world. I am allergic to latex, and I often employ the technique of "erasure" in my landscapes and portraits, using the locally manufactured product as well as prophylactic smocks, helmets, and gloves made from Indiana lambs' skins. I paint piles of raw materials as I breathe in the raw air all around me.

# SANFORD KNOX, FABRICATION

Winesburg's two towers, I built them. WOWO, the clear channel radio station broadcasting the late-night smoky ramblings of Listo Fisher all the way to Florida. WEEP, the public television channel that runs only telethons that feature as premiums the contents of lost luggage left at the Winesburg Trailways Bus station. I built them. I attached the throbbing red red lights at their tops, strung the guy wires, soldered the joints at altitude. I swear the air is thinner up there. To this day the stations both broadcast annually my suicide. My headlong dive, 500 feet, from the last story of the WEEP array. It wasn't me, of course, but a mannequin in a jumpsuit. A joke. I thought. My dream. My dream to be on television, on radio, to be turned into an aerosol, a cloud of electrons and broadcast, a magnetic signature written on the gray lake effected Indiana sky, out into all that space.

# MARGO FOWLER, SAFETY PATROL

I find I cannot leave my corner. I find I cannot leave my corner even when the captain of the Safety Patrol yodels the sad off duty call. "Off Duty . . . ! Off Duty . . . !" I begin to take off my belt. I begin to cross the street, heading toward school. I look both ways. I look both ways. But then, but then I think I think: Maybe I should wait. Maybe there is still someone on his or her way. I need to be *here* here. I need to wait. Wait. Just in case. Just in case. I hear the captain's call echo away in the distance, a kind of mournful song, a kind of call to prayer.

# CONTRACTOR JOHNNIE RITCHIE DISCOVERS SOMETHING ABOVE THE DROP CEILINGS OF WINESBURG'S HALDEMAN ERLICHMAN INFIRMARY

It is always the case that when you start a renovation, thinking it will be easy to add a door or window, you discover the compromises and quick fixes the previous builder concocted on the fly years ago. Look here, you say, I am going to put a door right here where this window is, use the window's header for the header of the door, only to find there never was a header there. That's okay though. I will be able to retrofit, rig something up that will work more or less. So I wasn't too surprised when renovating the H&E Infirmary—already a hodgepodge of clinics, offices, wards, theaters, centers, and practice suites dating from the Nixon administration—to discover this ancient braid of pneumatic tubes woven around and through the buildings above the acoustical tiles. It seemed to have at one time worked, transporting charts and reports, scripts and the pills prescribed. It is hard to believe that this twisted system worked, that the little lozenges and their cargoes found their ways from one end of the place to another. I have yet to find the vacuum, the heart of the matter that drew the atmosphere out of the coiling tubes, coaxing the capsules hither and yon. Nor have I found the central switches, the junctions, the gates. They are there someplace, I guess. I am just following one lead or another as it telescopes through the chases behind the old plaster walls, between the joists in the floors, the girders in the ceiling. It is strange to think that once they moved through this mesh of circulatory arteries real blood in bags, through the branching branches, to some anemic or hemorrhaging patient waiting patiently, the PICC line already in place, the drip dripping, the slender gauge needle already inserted into a throbbing vein.

# ROSS TANGENT, U.S. ARMY RETIRED

Somebody's got to keep track of all this. I volunteer. I tend the flags. Every day, I am up before dawn, like Francis Scott Key on his boat in the bay, hauling my long-handled red Radio Flyer wagon behind my tricycle to all my stations—the Durkheim High School, the PO, the WOWO transmitter, the car dealership, the war memorials, all the graveyards and cemeteries. I live at the Legion, Post 13. I am its only surviving member, a Viet Nam veteran, retired sergeant major from the Old Guard, 3rd Infantry Regiment. A medic, I saw action at Duc Pho with the 4th Battalion. At night, I sleep in the big empty hall. I leave the bingo machines on, the soft glow a lucky night-light. It is there, it's the rusting Quonset hut on the north side, where each morning I hoist the first flag of the day. I time it so on my transistor radio the anthem they play on the Little Red Barn show accompanies me. It is the last flag I lower and stow at the end of the day. Down in Fort Wayne, they leave their flags flying all the time, rain and shine. Oh sure, some of the places try to light them up at night to show some respect but that's not right. By law there are only a few places in the whole country where flags can be flown continuously. There's Fort McHenry, for sure, and the house in Baltimore where the Banner was made. The Iwo Jima statue, the Green in Lexington, The White House, Washington Monument, the Arch at Valley Forge and Custom Houses at ports of entry. That's it. All the rest is disrespectful if not downright illegal and just plain wrong. So each night I retrace my steps and haul in what I hoisted that morning, putting the flags to bed before I bed down in the recliner in the game room at Post 13. "Taps," I'm told, had something to do with shutting off the alcohol at the end of the day. They used to ship sailors home in casks of spirits or so I remember.

I remember when this place was jumping. The Falstaff and Old Crown flowed. Now, nothing to steep in but the silence. The wind seeping in through the chalking. I wrap myself up in the old flags at night when it is cold. I burn the wore out ones right here, inside, to stay warm.

# THE CITY MANAGER: THE TRANSFORMERS OF WINESBURG

There seems to be an inordinate amount of failure in Winesburg of pole positioned step-down transformers. In ordinary cases one would suspect the errant squirrel or random branch. But reconstructions of the outages fail to produce any evidence for such occult disruptions. It would be nice to find the carcass of a rodent or two, telltale sign of charcoal. But no. By all indications these explosions appear to be spontaneous, and they are persistent. Block after block go out nightly, occurring at dusk in the gloaming. It is akin to the current theories of infant colic that postulates the child, after a trying day of nervously wiring a nervous system for locomotion or communication collapses in the dark, the newly minted and fragile synapses snapping, the whole tenuous system giving up the ghost, so to speak, melting down into a fussy and inconsolable puddle. There is something, too, about the magnetic fields hereabouts. The northern lights can often be seen on the southern edge of city. There is the theory as well that Rea Magnet Wire has wired the town, using its grid to field-test new alloys for cable and experimental insulation sleeves. Perhaps there is something in the ground that prevents the proper grounding. The high-tension electricity leaks. At night, we have grown used to the pop, pop, pop of the transformers transforming, the heavy defeated breakers thumping home in the distant substations, that flickering light, and, then, that sudden but all too familiar darkness.

# CONSTANCE H. WOOTIN

Every morning, I call Elmer Xi, the undertaker at Jonesing Funereal Funerals (I have his number on speed dial), and ask him who's died overnight. And he tells me. I keep track, too, through the obituaries in the Fort Wayne papers, the South Bend and Columbia City ones as well. I like the obituary pages for their pictures, of course, but also for the body copy of the printed columns, gleaned from the mad lib templates (more often than not provided by Xi or one of his sons) for the bereaved survivors to complete. The whole surviving family constructs, on the spot, a family tree, a history, a biography. But it's the picture I like. And to run a picture in the obituary pages costs extra, I understand. It's the picture I need, and that picture is the picture the family paperclips to the scribbled form. It is either the only picture of the deceased or the one that everyone agreed looked most like the face they wanted to remember. It's his or her aspect in the after-life. His or her Heaven Face, I call it. The one that will be plastered on his or her for all eternity.

Most people think that the old murals they see in old post offices were painted by out-of-work artists, hired by the WPA (if they can even recall that alphabet agency), during the Great Depression. Mere make-work for hard times, they think. That's not quite correct.

The Winesburg post office was a standard design for 1934, a scaled down Greek temple on the outside with fluted columns and smooth limestone stone walls quarried in Bedford, Indiana, where you can see the quarrying of the blocks of Bedford limestone for the Winesburg PO depicted on the mural in the Bedford PO.

» » « «

All those murals are in all those lobbies. Terrazzo floors. Walnut trim. The three walls (not the wall with the front doors) have the windows where the clerks work and the rest is bricked with the tarnished PO box doors. Each door is studded with combination locks, knobs that spin a pointer from letter to letter inscribed above the little glass window with the golden decaled number.

I was born in Winesburg in 1930. The first thing I remember is the lobby of the PO. My mother brought me to the lobby and showed me the picture on the stamp she bought. It was a picture of a woman sitting in a chair. The stamp was all pink, the image etched on the paper of the stamp in pink whorls. My mother told me the stamp pictured a painting of an artist's mother. She showed me how to lick the stamp. I remember her pink tongue behind the pink stamp licking its back. She showed me how to stick the stamp to the big white envelope. She let me lick another stamp she tore from a sheet of stamps. I tried to see my tongue lick the glue. The glue tasted like glue.

On the wall to the right of the mail slot mother pushed the mail through was the massive scaffolding, the only thing in the brand new lobby not neat and orderly. It was rickety even then when it was new. It had been thrown together as the building was built, lattices and buttresses and cross-bucks and beams that made some room around the Postmaster's door (it said so on the fogged glass and still does: POSTMASTER). There was a man up on top of the nest of the scaffolding, sitting on an egg that wasn't really an egg but a paint can of white paint. He was looking closely at the blank wall way up there.

The PO murals weren't make-work so much as advertisements. President Roosevelt wanted to signal to the towns and villages that the federal government would, from now on, have a new relationship with its citizens. Times had changed. The post office had been the only US agency with which most people had any connection. So the new post offices were post offices for the people, for everyone. And the post offices would have stories to tell.

I am over eighty years old. I have an electric lift that lifts me up to the top of the scaffolding. It is always warmer up here, right under the ceiling and the sweet odor the plaster puts out as it evaporates seems to drape itself over, like laundry on a line, the fret work of cables and struts, turnbuckles and guy wires that support the paint splattered platform. A real drapery of 6 mil Visqueen shapes the vapors, a thin atmosphere of thinner that has been circulating here for forever. No one below can see how the mural is going. It is in progress, has been in progress since 1934. The only post office mural in the Winesburg PO begun in the Great Depression is the only post office mural that has never been finished. While other murals are restored or are removed or discovered under coats of plaster that are seared away by means of laser beams, this mural inhabits another state altogether, suspended. Suspended, as I am suspended floating on these persistent clouds of dank water and wet lime here in the lobby near the ceiling of the Winesburg PO.

The mural is a fresco mural so each day I apply a new wash of lime mortar and begin to paint, injecting the pigment in the drying plaster. As the wall sweats and squeezes out its moisture, I can feel the coolness glaze my cheek. I'm an old woman, nearly blind now. I am right on top of the painting even though I have several layers of loupes and lenses and magnifying glasses wired to my head. I lick the point of my brush to shape its point. I taste dirt in all its colors. I taste seaweed and the sea. I taste bones and shells. I taste iodine. I taste lead.

» » « «

The man in my memory up on the scaffolding painting the wall, that was Bart Harz, the painter originally hired to tell the story of Winesburg in the PO's mural. The artists back then were encouraged to depict an historical moment in the murals, celebrate native crops or manufactured goods, capture a geographical feature, or feature an ethnic or cultural peculiarity. Color the local color.

For years, as we stood in line, waiting to approach the clerk's window for service, we would look up to Bart, sitting on the platform near the ceiling, staring at the big empty wall. Or mailing a letter, flipping the flap door a time or two to make sure the letter slid down the chute, we would turn and say to Bart, "How's it going, Bart?" Or dialing the combination of the boxes and sorting out the day's mail, we would ponder Bart pondering on his perch. It was hard to leave the lobby after awhile. You wanted to linger just a moment more. And then a moment more. And then another moment to see if, right then Bart would, at that moment, apply the first brush stroke. You didn't want to miss it. Or, at least, see him begin to sketch, trace out a gesture with a piece of charcoal. This went on for years.

There is plenty of paint on the wall in front of me now. There is too much paint. Layers and layers of it. I am constantly revising the faces in the fresco as the faces they are modeled on change and grow older. I must slather on a new skim coat each day. Each day draw the hairlines back a little farther on the men whose hairlines are receding. Or gray the hair on the ones whose hair is graying. Change the color of the hair on those who've changed the color of their hair. Redo the styles as the styles go in and out of fashion, document this haircut or that, and, every spring, get ready to coif the prom hair-dos for that spring's junior girls at Durkheim High. And that's just the hair. There is the clothing to do. The glasses that have moved to bifocals, trifocals. Hats and gloves have mostly disappeared. The dollop of sparkle that represents an engagement ring, wedding ring and then in some cases, painting over the rings. Shades of lipstick. The skin itself reflects the seasons—the summer's bronze tan, the lake effect's pale pale. I add the wrinkle here. The age spot there. A scar or two. I work hard to paint a patch of a palsy creeping over a face.

"How's it going, Constance?" I hear someone shout to me from below. I wave over my shoulder. It goes, I think, it goes.

During lunch, I sit on the platform dangling my feet out over the lobby. I peel back all of my optics, revealing my naked eyes. I watch the citizens of Winesburg below doing their postal business. Jim Hitch is going out of town. Charlie Kimble has a notice that there is something too big to fit in his box. Wanda Weintraub asks for a duck stamp. Omar B Wells, there is no period after the B, has a package to mail to his sister in Peoria. Johnson Jr. is filling out his selective service form. And Sallie Nadir is showing little Josh how to peel a stamp, the Liberty Bell, from the booklet she just bought and apply it to a letter his mother then slides in the slot. Josh looks back up to me looking down at him. He sticks out his tongue. I stick out mine.

Bart never painted a lick of paint. Ever since Mother showed me the picture of the painting of a mother on that stamp, I have wanted to be an artist. When Mother realized that she took me back to the PO and asked Bart to give me lessons in drawing, painting, composition when he took breaks from his not-working work. He needed the money, he said, and he needed the break from the break that, up until he started teaching me, looked pretty much like what he was doing when not on break. I sat on an up-ended unopened paint can in the middle of the PO's lobby and sketched Bart as he worked or, more accurately, as he didn't work. Charcoal and pastels, washes and inks, pencil and pen and brush, watercolors, oils. I even did a pointillistic collage out of pictures I snipped from LIFE magazine, now dead. He'd have me help him rebuild his scaffold. I would re-rig the poles and platforms, the struts and the netting. The airy scrim that hung from the ceiling like a cloud. I would sketch Bart and the scaffold and the PO boxes and the empty wall, the white whiteness of it stretching on and on behind him.

All those studies prepared me to fill in for Bart Harz after he bit the dust after the War. The commission came to me, a codicil to his will. I was bequeathed the rigging and the rigmarole in rigor mortis all those years. The dried up paint, all those shades of blue, the thinners and the pigments, the dry points and the abandoned stencils, the masking tape and the spent snap lines. I was willed the pots and kidney-shaped French palettes with their histories of miscalculated mixing, rainbows of mud and dung derivations, and the wall, I inherited the empty wall and its fifteen years of priming, priming, priming, priming.

That wall is filled with faces now, a portrait of everyone in town, and each of those faces I touch up each day, age them and gray them, add the wide-eyed new arrivals and close the eyes of the citizens who have died as if a camera has caught them blinking in the sun not sleeping for eternity. It is a field in which the populace of Winesburg is arrayed and the field has depth of field and the folks in the further back ranks shrink in that illusion of distance, dwindle to the distant vanishing point. Some face no bigger than this "o" here and with my skill of shading and a triple aught brush I contour even that minute visage with the expressions of joy and wonder.

》　》　《　《

They are all looking up. They are looking up to Bart on his jury-rigged tower, his back to the PO lobby below. It is all tromp l'oeil, and Bart is bent to his work painting the people of Winesburg spread out before him in attitudes of joy and wonder looking back at the artist who is rendering them so effortlessly and with such detail.

And there, there I am on my paint can stool, an egg, looking over Bart's soft cotton shoulder. I am in profile, depicted as some antique muse, attempting to sketch the artist's, Bart's, own profile I alone can see. It seems I am whispering into his ear, a flash of a pearl pink tongue, a kind of spark between the synapses, rendered between my lips. Still wet, the image glistens. I dismantle all my lenses and glasses and goggles. I lean into this point of paint, the picture closing in on me. And with my own tongue, I tongue the image of my tongue, taste it, that metal taste, that taste of earth, that taste of pink. And with my tongue I draw out the tongue-shaped image of my tongue in the fresco. Shape it. Give it depth and texture. I lap and flick. I am blind to it. It is all by feel. This final touch. This articulation. This accent. This annunciation.

But I myself, I will leave unfinished. A kind of spirit, a ghost. I am an impression, impasto. A blur really. A bunch of hasty gestures, smudged lines, and smeared paints in unsubtle hues. I float like a cloud, undone, my gossamer gown's draping all hurried and fudged, naive, here all flat, stiff, matte. My face, except for around the mouth, a blank, traced, an empty outline, still waiting to be finished, sealed, fixed, done after all these years, done. Finally finished after I have completed all of my studies of this little precinct of this unending, this infinite, heaven.

# IT TAKES A VILLAGE

First, I must thank the Ways & Means committee at Baobab Press for laying the ground work for this new album, *Plain Air: Sketches from Winesburg, Indiana*: Christine E. Kelly Publisher & Executive Editor, and Danilo John Thomas Managing Editor & Prose editor. I am so grateful that they felt at home in these pages and provided these pages a home.

The town of Winesburg, Indiana, began as a postcard project, a collection of quick sketches, as the centennial of Sherwood Anderson's landmark collection, *Winesburg, Ohio*, approached. I thank Bryan Furuness and Robert Stapleton editors at *Booth*, a journal published by Butler University's Creative Writing MFA Program, for securing the land grant for me to begin to populate the town with tales of its inhabitants. Bryan and I then used my original contributions as seed to create a hybrid anthology made up of my stories and other stories set in Winesburg, conceived by other Hoosier and Midwestern writers. *Winesburg, Indiana*, was published in 2015, by Break Away Books, an imprint of Indiana University Press, and I would like to thank the editors there, Linda Oblack and Sarah Jacobi for the fertile ground and Brian McMullen for the remarkable cover art. I thank, too, the civil engineers who continued the build with their original stories: Barbara Bean, Kate Bernheimer, Robin Black, Karen Brennan, Brian Buckbee, Shannon Cain, Sherrie Flick, Roxane Gay, B. J. Hollars, C. J. Hribal, Andrew Hutchins, Sean Lovelace, Lee Martin, Erin McGraw, Valerie Miner, Kelcey Evick Parker, Edward Porter, Ethel Rohan, Valerie Sayers, Greg Schwipps, Porter Shreve, George Singleton, Deb Olin Unferth, Jim Walker, and Claire Vaye Watkins.

》　》　《　《

"The gift moves towards the empty place. As it turns in its circle it turns towards him who has been empty-handed the longest, and if someone appears elsewhere whose need is greater it leaves its old channel and moves toward him. Our generosity may leave us empty, but our emptiness then pulls gently at the whole until the thing in motion returns to replenish us. Social nature abhors a vacuum."

— Lewis Hyde,
*The Gift: Imagination and the Erotic Life of Property*

Besides Winesburg, Indiana, I've lived in many cities & towns. In one place I lived, Cambridge, I was able to write with Lewis Hyde, who I thank here for that writing and for the notion that art, constantly in motion, moves us and moves through us to bind us all together in creative gift communities. In Cambridge and Medford, I also thank other writers who I wrote with and still write for: Nancy Esposito, David Rivard, Monroe Engel, Christopher Leland, Osvaldo Sabino, Susan Dodd, Verlyn Klinkenborg, Jonathan Strong, Julia Dubner, Heather Gunn, Mike Mattison, Jim Marino, Noah Bly, Monica Hileman, and Emily Barton.

In Ames, Story County, and Iowa, the gift still moves through Joe Geha and Fern Kupfer, Mary Howard, Marilyn Sandidge, Steve Pett and Clare Cardinal, Mary Swander, Jane Smiley, Rosanne Potter and Bill McCarthy, Sam Pritchard and Tista Simpson, Neil Nakadate, Marlis Manley, Dale Ross, Susan Carlson, Jennie Ver Steeg, Steve Gulick, Jane Dupuis, Eric and Ross Brown, Anne Hunsinger, Allan Schmidt, Brian Meyer, David Hamilton, Kathy Hall, Ori Fienberg and Emily Maloney, Rachel Yoder, Chinelo Okparanta, Jenny Colville, Robin Hemley, Zach Vickers, Dylan Nice, Allen Gee, Michael Lewis-Beck, Rick Moody and Laurel Nakadate, Amy Margolis, and Jan Weissmiller.

In darkest Syracuse with only 60 days a year of available sunlight, the gift was lit by Melanie Rae Thon, Safiya

Henderson-Holmes, John Crowley, Margaret Himley, Bruce Smith, Del Lausa, Lisa Howard, John McKenzie, Danit Brown, Steven Featherstone, David Keith, Steve Fellner, M.T. Anderson, Marilyn Winkler, Roberta Bernstein, Vincent Standley, Heidi Lynn Staples, David Rossman, Betsy Hogan, Chris Riley and Mark Feldman, Roger Hecht, Ajay Bhatt, Jen Reeder and Bryan Fryklund, Paul Germano, Matt Dube, Jane Binns, Chris Kennedy, Cheryl Dumesnil, and Paul Maliszewski.

In Swannanoa where I would take up temporary residency for 10-day stretches each winter and summer in the 80s and 90s, I knit together a little community with the aid of the United States Postal Service. I am so grateful for the ongoing give and take Cynthia Reeves, Lisa van Orman Hadley, Judy French, Rachel Howard, Samantha Hunt, Sarah Buttenwieser, Helen Fremont, Achy Obejas, Kathleen Collissen, Elizabeth Mosier, Matthew Simmons, Catherine Brown, Fred Arroyo, Sara Harrell, Charles Baxter, Natalie Harris, Peter Turchi, and Peggy Shinner.

179

In Tuscaloosa below the Bug Line, I settled in and have lived here for more than a quarter century where I wrote with a remarkable cadre of writers in old Mildew Hall including Kellie Wells, Patti White, Brian Oliu, Robin Behn, Yolanda Manora, Hank Lazer, Lex Williford, Peter Streckfus and Heather Green, Dave Madden, Kate Bernheimer (who I have thanked above) and Joyelle McSweeney (to whom this book is dedicated), Hali Felt, L. Lamar Wilson, Don Belton, Wilton Barnhardt, and Sandy Huss. In the 25 years I've lived in Alabama, I welcomed and said goodbye to a whole slew of writers who moved to Tuscaloosa to write for four years and create their own creative communities. I attempted to catalogue them here, to thank them all, but it began to look like a credit crawl at the end of a CGI movie—perfunctory, rote, nearly 300 names. Still, I thank you all, each and everyone. You know who you are. And all y'all are more than the list you left. The University here requires that I include on each syllabus my "expected outcome" for the class, and I always indicate that my "expected outcome" was that "in 20 years my students would still be writing." The Dean, confused, called me in and asked how I would "assess" this. I answered by saying I would give them a call in 20 years to "assess the outcome." I had the answer already in any case. The gift keeps flowing. I didn't really have to call because I've stayed in touch. They've sent me their books of stories and poems, letters, cards, words and pictures, a moving movable metropolis of writers writing, giving gifts to the wider and wider world and receiving my welling and ever endless gratitude.

I want to thank my hubbubing buddies, co-counselors who confab monthly on all things bookish and beyond, the founders and foundation of fellowship: Dan Waterman, Steve Davis, Lee Pike, Randy Fowler, Billy Field, David Allgood, Tom Fletcher, Hobson Bryan, Jim Merrell, Bob Lyman, and Sam Rombokas.

I thank my veteran maintenance-of-way crew team members, the street-sweepers, the night watchmen flame-keepers: Susan Neville, Michael Rosen, Ann Jones, Michael Wilkerson (retired), John Barth, Scott Sanders, Maureen Pilkington, Jeremy Butler, Louise Erdrich, Jay Brandon, Dan Zweig, Bob and Lori Sullivan, Dan Cooreman, Rikki Ducornet, and Marian Young, the first first responder.

Back home in Indiana, right down the road from Winesburg, the murmuring suburbs of my heart: Tim, Amy, Ben, and Gina Martone; Wayne, Ruth, and Andy Payne; Linda Dibblee; Dawn Burns; Robert and Irene Walters.

Thank you to Sam, Stella, and Nick, who make the passages possible, locks and dams who lift me everyday.

As always this is for Theresa, the prime surveyor (theodolite & chain) of my metaphors, who gives to me, in detailed maps, all the terrestrial, three-dimensional position points, the distances, and the angles between them, that is to say, every crease, the interlocking grid, and who makes the whole wide world we inhabit.

# ACKNOWLEDGEMENTS

"The City Manager: An Introduction"; "Ken of Ken's Camera"; "Susan App, Truancy Secretary"; "Cantor Quadruplets"; "Leslie Sanguine"; "Cafeteria Cashier"; "Howard Junker, Facilities Engineer"; "Carl Franken-stein, Custodian"; "Carol Clay"; "Greg Pittman"; and "Constance H. Wooten" originally appeared in *Booth Magazine* and then were collected in *Winesburg, Indiana*, edited by Michael Martone and Bryan Furuness and pub-lished by Break Away Books in 2015. They are gratefully reprinted here with permission granted by Indiana Uni-versity Press.

Many of these sketches appeared first in the following magazines and journals, in print and online. I am grateful to Robert Stapleton of *Booth*, Josh Russell of *Five Points*, Erin Stalcup of *Hunger Mountain*, Kim Chinquee of *Elm Leaves Journal*, Gabriel Blackwell of *The Rupture* (fka *The Collagist*), Edward Byrne of *Valparaiso Fiction Re-view*, and Jane Huffman of *Guesthouse*.

"Marvin Puff Motors"; "Kendra Klein, Buddhist"; "Al-ice Tang, Competitive Clothespin Pinner"; "The 141st Acoustic Battalion (Early's Ears), Indiana National Guard"; "Simon Gluck, Midget Racer Racer"; "The Winesburg Bleachatorium"; "The Hotel Fort Wayne"; "The Windmill Garden"; "The Paint Testing Fields"; "Seth Pollin's White Elephant"; "Plein Air Painter"; "Sanford Knox, Fabrication"; and "Margo Fowler, Safety Patrol" appeared in *Buta: A Paragraphiti Anthology*, ed-ited by Joyelle McSweeney and Valerie Sayers as "Dis-patches from Winesburg, Indiana".

"Brandon Zweig's Life Preserver"; "Drake Cast, Ground Crew"; "Gail Tingle's Horse Trough"; "The Abandoned Floss Factory"; "Juan Reyes, Lineman"; "Gloria Gleason's Crocheted Pennants"; "Klaus Weber, Curb House Numberer"; and "Janet Vachon's Glider" first appeared online at *The Collagist*, which has since been renamed *The Rupture*.

"Tab Gallenbeck, Public Works"; "The Snow Fences of Winesburg"; "Bud's Komet's Puck"; "Bobbi Bodinka's Rubbings"; "Thursday"; "The Lamar Sign on the Old Lincoln Highway"; and "Sandor Reeves's Extension Cord" were originally published in *Elm Leaves Journal: Dirt*.

"The Plumanns Sisters' Lustron House"; "Margaret Wiggs's Due Date Stamp"; "Ned Shoots the Sun"; "My Grandfather's Riddle"; "Clayton Tang, Business Sign Painter"; "Ernestina Stevens, Hydrologist Poet"; "The Winesburg Y"; "Techniques for Painting Eyes"; "Patty Pane, Horticulturalist"; "Fred Burke, Name Tag Recycler"; "The Historically Preserved Telephone Booth of Winesburg, Indiana"; "Glynis Smart's Wooden Ice Cream Spoon"; "Graham Walter's Fighting Kites Are Fighting"; "Someone is Painting the Elm Trees of Winesburg"; and "Alexandria Flowers Takes Her Limbic System for a Walk" were originally published by *Five Points* and won that magazine's Paul Bowles Prize.

"Jimmie D'Angelo's Observatory"; "Detective Sgt. Gabbie Cline, Indiana State Police"; "Zeke Remke, Fishing Lure Maker"; "Gary Franke's Fan"; and "Sigrid Starr, Server, The Huddle House" first appeared in *Florida Review*.

"The County Extension Agency's Experimental Bamboo Plot"; "My Flat Top"; "Ron's Lawn Roller"; and "A Deep Fat Fried Breaded Pork Tenderloin from John's Awful Awful (Awful Good, Awful Big)" first appeared, in a slightly different form, in *Guesthouse*.

"Mario Talarico's Peonies"; "Maurice Milkin, Eraser Carver"; "Sue Johnson, Parking Enforcement Officer"; and "The Weeping Willow Windbreak of Winesburg" were originally published by *Hunger Mountain*.

"Deb Sanders's Etch-A-Sketches"; "Jim O'Day's Folly"; and "My Grandfather's Hog Oiler" appeared first in *Inscape*.

"Flegler's Interior Design" was first published in *Memorious*.

"The Transformers of Winesburg" and "Dan Howell Building The Great Wall of Winesburg" were originally published in *Mesmer*.

"Archeology Is a Kind of Destruction" and "My Family's Velvet Ropes" appeared first in *Midwest Review*.

"The Winesburg Cancer Center"; "Amy Margolis's Pile of Lights"; and "Blanche's Aluminum Ice Cube Tray" first appeared in *Mississippi Review*.

"Claude Burke Swan Boating on the Fork River"; "The Biomet Seconds Outlet"; "Forrest Norton, Camera Operator, Google Street View"; "The Mosquito Truck of Winesburg"; "Picky Dashner, Slow Pour Oil Change"; and "Carrie Crabtree, Pawpaw Grower" were originally published by *North American Review*.

"Things"; "The Girlhood Home of Zerna Sharp"; "The Flyway of Blue Trucks"; "Contractor Johnnie Ritchie Discovers Something Above the Drop Ceilings of Winesburg's Haldeman & Erlichman Infirmary"; "Hunter and Art Hunt, Student Fund Raisers"; and "Ross Tangent, U.S. Army Retired" first appeared in *Pretty Owl Poetry*.

"The Dead Mall" was a finalist in the World's Greatest Short Short Fiction Contest at Florida State University and was published in *Southeast Review*.

"The Winesburg Motor Speedway"; "Captain Steve 'Even' Steven, 122nd Wing Indiana Air National Guard"; "The Drinking Fountain in Throw Park"; "The Winesburg Moist Towelette Company"; and "Found in Gabriel Wichern's Backyard" originally appeared in *Talking River.*

"Van Zimmer's Tree Zoo"; "The Annual Metal Detector Migration"; and "The National Mourners Union, Local 440" first appeared in *Threadcount.*

"Nikki Temone, PBX Operator, The Gerber Haus Motel" was first published in *Tupelo Quarterly.*

"Ruel Coal & Ice"; "Sunset Contrail Viewing"; "The Bat Boxes of Winesburg, Indiana"; "Carson Carlson, Linoleum Installer"; "The County Extension Agent"; and "Zandor Sands, Homeowner" first appeared in *Valparaiso Fiction Review.*

# MICHAEL MARTONE, HYBREDIZING HYBREDIZER

Michael Martone was born in Fort Wayne, Indiana. Growing up in Indiana, a teenaged Martone, along with many of his age-mates, took summertime employment in the agricultural sector of the state's economy. It was a rite of passage to ride the mechanical carriers through the extensive seed cornfields that surrounded the nearby small town of Winesburg, Indiana, detasseling the plant in order to produce hybridized strains of the grain. Martone enjoyed drifting above the tasseling plants, the ocean of vinyl green corn, a vortex swirling around him. He usually worked in fields planted in 4:1 panels, four female rows of one variety to be detasseled and one bull row left to pollinate. The blocks created a wavy pattern in the fields he sailed over, carefully unspooling the threads of the tassels from the tangle of leaves the machines had missed. At other times he rouged as well, walking the shaded rows searching for the volunteer starts and preventing their undesirable pollen from taking root in the precious hybridizing. At night, after the long day of gleaning every strand from every plant, Martone would dream he was a dusty bee or a caked butterfly, staggering from one forest of tassels to the next into the chromatic confusion of the morning. And in the fall, after school had started up again, he returned to the now harvested fields, the sharp stubble laced with frost, and huddled under the scratchy wool blankets in the back of an old buckboard bumping through the empty fields near the small town of Winesburg, a passenger on one of the last real hayrides in Indiana, and whispered to the girl beside him the intricate secrets of the intriguing sex life of corn.

Michael Martone's most recent books are *The Complete Writings of Art Smith, The Bird Boy of Fort Wayne, Edited by Michael Martone* and *Brooding*, essays. After forty years of teaching at universities and colleges, he retired in 2020. He lives in Tuscaloosa, Alabama.